# Almost Sleighed

## Maple Syrup Mysteries Book 3

### Emily James

Stronghold Books
ONTARIO, CANADA

*For my grandma. All my weird parts come from her, and I mean that as a compliment. Those are some of my favorite parts.*

*A lie gets halfway around the world before the truth has a chance to put its pants on.*

– WINSTON CHURCHILL

# Chapter 1

When I'd imagined my life growing up, I'd never envisioned being out in a sugar bush in Michigan, covered in gooey maple sap. I didn't even like the cold, and if there was one thing Michigan was in late February, it was cold.

Then again, there were currently a lot of things about my life that I never would have guessed as a kid could possibly happen to me—like how many times in the past six months someone had tried to kill me, for example.

I followed the loud hissing noise, like an angry winterized cobra, to the nearest powder-blue sap line. The hole in this one was so large that the sap dripped from the bottom like my trees were bleeding out on the ground.

"Found another one," I called back over my shoulder to Russ, Sugarwood's manager and my guru when it came to all things maple syrup production.

Had I been alone in figuring out how to run the maple syrup farm my Uncle Stan left me, I wouldn't have known what to do when we turned on the vacuum pump this morning to start the sugaring season and barely a dribble of sap moved from our lines into the holding tank. Russ immediately put together teams and sent us out looking for frozen, broken, or leaking pipes. We knew the sap was running, so we had to be losing it somewhere along the way.

"Catch," Russ called.

I spun around in time for a roll of silver duct tape to fly by my head and into a snow drift. My Great Dane puppy and aging Bullmastiff barreled past me after it as if Russ had thrown a ball instead.

Russ waddled toward me, his barrel-shaped body rocking awkwardly back and forth on his snowshoes. "Did you play *any* sports as a kid?"

I could almost hear my parents laughing hysterically all the way from Virginia. "When my class was rowdy in elementary school, I used to hope the teacher punished us by canceling gym class, if that tells you anything."

My Great Dane puppy already had one paw planted on the roll of duct tape, holding it down while she gnawed on it. I wriggled it from her grip. She'd only managed to leave a couple of holes so far, which was better than some of my belongings were faring through the teething stage.

I handed the tape back to Russ. "We might want to use a fresh roll until this one dries."

He accepted it with two fingers and a grimace. "This is our last one. Noah was supposed to bring out more, and a couple new fittings, too."

We'd already gone through the repair supplies we'd carried out with us, and Russ had called back to Sugarwood on his walkie-talkie for more. But that was thirty minutes ago. Unless Noah got lost in the bush—and the man had better directional skills than a search-and-rescue dog, so I doubted it—he should have been here by now. With all the teams we sent out, he might have received a more urgent call from one of the others, though.

More faint hissing came from behind me, signaling that the leak we were standing beside wasn't the only one near us. "Is this amount of damage normal even after we already walked the lines?"

Russ wiped the roll on his pant leg and wound the tape around the piping. "That was only looking for major damage. You can't always see the small damage from woodpeckers and squirrels until the sap starts to run."

That hadn't actually answered my question, but the extra creasing around Russ' normally jovial mouth and eyes did. For some reason, our lines were abnormally compromised.

I opened my mouth to ask him what this might mean for our syrup production and profit margin, but he'd pulled out his walkie-talkie again and had the button depressed.

"Looking for an ETA on those supplies, Noah. Over." He released the button, but the line stayed quiet. "Anyone got eyes on Noah? Over."

The replies popcorned in. All negative.

Russ pulled out his cell phone. His small head shake telegraphed the lack of signal. Fair Haven, with all its dead zones, often felt like it belonged back in the 90s.

Russ ruffled his grey hair with a sticky hand, like he'd forgotten the sap was there. His hair stood up in spikes.

A knotty ball formed in my chest. Russ' actions said this was about more than just the need for parts. The question was whether he was fretting about the impact of the delay on our season or about Noah. "You seem worried."

I tried to keep my voice casual. Russ tended to glue his lips together when it came to anyone else's business. If he felt like I was pushing him at all, I'd get nothing from him. And it wasn't that I wanted to be nosy, but if one of my employees was having a serious enough issue for Russ to agonize about it, it seemed like something I should know.

His expression smoothed out, but not completely, making it even more obvious that what he felt inside wasn't what he wanted reflected. "I wanted your first season to start off better, is all. Maybe I'll head back and check on Noah."

I was the best choice to go back to Sugarwood and find a cell signal to call Noah. Compared to Russ, my skills in finding and fixing leaks in the lines were similar to the Karate Kid vs. Mr. Miyagi. "I'll go. I wanted to take the dogs back anyway so they can get warmed up."

Russ shifted his weight back and forth. He clearly knew that if he argued with me, I'd want a reason. Finally, he nodded. "Give me a call on the walkie-talkie when you're headed back out."

I'd have to let it drop for now and hope Russ would confide in me if it was something I should know about.

I called for the dogs. Toby came immediately. Velma snaked along, heading in my direction but taking the opportunity to smell everything.

Russ did a double-take as she passed. "Are her toenails blue?"

"I got tired of people calling her a *him*, so I painted them." I clipped on their leashes. "I have purple and pink, too."

The look he gave me said *crazy lady*. I gave him a cheeky grin and headed back toward the buildings. What was the point in having dogs if you didn't have fun with them?

As soon as I neared the tree line, my phone caught a signal. I dialed Noah. It rang through to voicemail.

The knot in my chest swelled. I should have pressed Russ to tell me why he was acting funny. Now I was coming up with all sorts of crazy ideas in my head, starting with Noah having collapsed in the store due to a brain tumor.

His voicemail told me to leave a message.

"Hey, it's Nicole. Call me. Russ is worried about you, and we need those supplies."

I walked the dogs back to my house and tucked them into the laundry room together, then headed along the path to the sugar shack. If Noah had his hands full fixing a piece of equipment, he wouldn't have been able to answer. I'd eliminate the most likely causes for this delay before I let my suspicious mind run amuck.

No one at the sugar shack had seen him since we discovered the sap wasn't flowing in properly, but his truck was parked out front, a case of duct tape and a couple plastic bags emblazoned with DAD'S HARDWARE STORE on the seat.

There was only one other place I could think of that he might be. He could have gone to hook up the two Clydesdales we used to pull the sleigh for tours, planning to bring the supplies out to everyone that way. He liked to use the horses as much as possible to keep them in practice.

I passed the spot where our antique sugar shack had burned down. The snow covered the charred ring now, which made it easier to pretend that the spot had always been empty. Russ said we'd rebuild come spring and hopefully we wouldn't lose too many tour bookings. The original sugar shack had been a big draw, especially for families and school groups.

Our stable sat on the other side of the clearing. The sliding door hung open.

The tension melted from my shoulders. The delay was just Noah bringing out the horses. I'd pop my head in anyway. I wanted to learn every aspect of the business, and even though Noah had been giving me lessons in handling and tacking the horses, I was still a novice.

I stepped through the doorway and slid my sunglasses up onto the top of my head. The stable had that warm smell of horses and hay. Before I'd ever experienced it, I'd assumed I'd hate the "stinky" smell of a stable. Instead, it'd ended up feeling like being wrapped up in a warm blanket, that same sense of comfort and security.

A funny undertone hung in the air today though. I couldn't identify it over the other familiar smells. A headache pricked the back of my eyes.

The horses were still in their stalls, and Noah wasn't in sight, but he could be back in the tack room. His toolbox sat next to Key's stall. "Noah? Are you in here?"

One of the horses snorted, and I moved over to the nearest stall. I called both Leaf and his younger brother, Key, my "gentle giants." They weighed over 2000 pounds each, and their backs were well over my head, but they were calm even around screaming babies, which was more than I could say for me.

Leaf stayed at the back of his stall instead of coming forward to nuzzle me for carrot bits. My only experience with horses was with these two that I'd inherited, but Leaf looked off to me. There was extra white in his eyes, and his ears swiveled. His upper lip curled almost like he was tasting the air.

He could be smelling the same out-of-place smell that I did, or he could be sick. I didn't know enough about horses to tell. "Noah?"

I leaned sideways so I could see Key in the next stall. He snorted again—the first one must have come from him. They were both acting weird, so at least it wasn't likely that Leaf was sick. We'd already had enough trouble with the lines. A sick horse was the last thing we needed.

I dialed Noah's number again. His ringtone sounded from Key's stall.

My fingers went cold despite my thick gloves. He wouldn't have been so careless as to have dropped his phone in the stall, but I should be able to see him if he were in there. Unless he wasn't on his feet.

What I wanted to do was run back outside and pretend I'd never come to the barn. What I wanted to do was call Russ and wait for him to join me.

What I needed to do was look. I crept forward, stood on my tiptoes, and peeked over the door.

Noah lay in the wood shavings on the floor of the stall, covered in blood.

# Chapter 2

I dialed 9-1-1 and explained to the woman who
answered where I was and what I'd found.

"I'm sending the police and an ambulance," the
operator said. "Are you able to tell if he's breathing?"

The same shudder as when I walked into a spider
web in the woods curled across my skin. Even after all
the bodies I'd seen in the past six months, I still wasn't
used to it. And this was Noah. He wasn't some
stranger.

But that's exactly why I needed to do it. Because it
was Noah, and I was responsible for him as his employer. If he was still alive, I should sit beside him and let
him know he wasn't alone in the minutes until help
arrived.

I unlatched the stall door and slipped inside. Key stayed to the back of the stall as if he understood that he needed to be careful not to step on Noah. Noah's chest rose and fell, but there was an awful lot of blood. My vision blurred.

No way was I passing out now. The emergency personnel didn't need to worry about me when they got here.

*Imagine the blood is red paint,* I told myself. *Lots and lots of red paint.*

I eased down beside Noah, stripped off my gloves, and took his hand. "Help is coming. Hang in there."

"Is he conscious?" the operator's voice asked in my ear.

"No, but I thought he might still be able to hear me."

The bulky key ring with a master set of keys that Noah always wore on his belt jabbed into my thigh. I wedged the phone between my cheek and my shoulder and shifted position. My hand landed in something gooey, and my stomach rolled.

"How far out are they?" I asked.

My voice had that weird, thready wobble to it that meant my brain and my body were about to get into a fight over whether I stayed upright or not.

"You should hear sirens any minute now."

The blare of a siren sounded, almost like I'd willed it into existence. My head cleared slightly.

I let the operator know they'd arrived and then disconnected. "I'm going to leave for just a minute," I told Noah. "I have to let them know where you are."

Whether talking to him did any good or not, the 9-1-1 operator hadn't acted like it was silly, so it couldn't hurt. And it was what I'd want someone to do for me. Some part of his brain might still be registering information.

I directed the ambulance and the woman officer who pulled into the clearing less than twenty seconds after. She glanced at my blood-covered hand but went inside anyway.

Then I was by myself with a hand covered in Noah's blood. My mind kept coming back to it like it was driving in circles. I knelt down and wiped off what I could in the snow. It left garish crimson streaks behind.

I turned my back to them and pulled the walkie-talkie from my belt. I needed Russ to come with me to the hospital, and if he knew anything about why this had happened, he had some explaining to do. Given how on edge he'd been about Noah's absence before, I was betting he wasn't as naïve as he'd wanted to appear.

I pressed the walkie-talkie's button. "Russ, this is Nicole. I need you back at the main buildings. Over."

As hard as I tried to control my tone, my voice came out sounding like a mom who'd found her child playing in the street, that unique combination of angry and terrified. That was going to be enough to ignite Fair

Haven's rumor mill all by itself. Hopefully the employees would assume it was another glip in production. I was the newbie, after all. No one would be surprised if all the problems we'd already had flustered me.

And since Russ had a predisposition toward discretion, hopefully he wouldn't ask what was wrong. The last thing I wanted to do was broadcast Noah's condition over the radio system for all our employees to hear.

"Where at? Over." The careful question let me know that he understood not to ask for more information right now.

"Out at the stable. Over."

"Excuse me, ma'am," a female voice said from behind me.

I turned back toward the stable. The EMTs rolled a stretcher out the double-wide door meant for the sleigh. Noah was strapped in, one EMT working on him as they moved. That was a good sign, right? They must think there was something they could do for him.

I moved after them, but the officer blocked my path.

She was tall for a woman, and I had to look up into her face. "Am I not allowed to go with him?"

"You can follow later, but it'll be better if you don't join him in the ambulance."

I leaned around her and watched as they loaded Noah. They kept the lights on and sped off. It was hard to watch them go and not be able to immediately follow.

Who would give them the emergency contact information for Noah's next of kin? And if Russ and I weren't there when the doctor spoke to his family, who knew how long we'd have to wait before we found out his condition. There'd been so much blood on the ground under him. What if he...

The blood on the snow drew my gaze again. The officer followed my gaze with her own.

Her face hardened into a wall of expressionless steel. The tight bun in her slicked-back black hair added to the impression of inflexibility. "I need to ask you a few questions."

Had Erik or Officer Quincey Dornbush been the one to respond to the call, they would have offered to talk somewhere away from the smear, but it seemed like a similar offer wouldn't be forthcoming today. In fact, from the way she stared me down, she felt a lot more like a foe than an ally. It was a relationship dynamic I should be used to after my time as a criminal defense attorney, but I wasn't a lawyer now. I was a distraught witness. And she already had a terrible crime-scene-side manner.

I'd be polite even if she wasn't going to show concern for me. Taking care of Noah and finding out how he ended up bleeding on the ground was more important than anything else.

"I'm happy to help," I said.

Her deadpan expression didn't even flicker into something closer to compassion. "That's an interesting choice of words. How about you tell me what happened."

Great. So that's how this was going to play out. As if the situation wasn't already bad enough, the responding officer wanted to look at me as a suspect because I'd used the word *happy*. Obviously I hadn't actually meant joyful.

The less defensive side of me said the blood on my hand and the fact that I'd been in such a hurry to wipe it off might have had something to do with it as well.

I went through a more detailed version of what I'd told the 9-1-1 operator. "Then I sat with him until I heard the sirens."

"Nicole!" Russ' voice called from across the clearing.

He hustled across the snow, looking a lot like a short-legged bulldog plowing his way along.

The female officer's face softened. "Hey, Russ. I was hoping the next time I saw you would be when I brought the kids for their yearly sleigh ride rather than under circumstances like this. I'm so sorry."

"Elise." Russ' words came out on an out-of-breath huff. "What happened?"

"It's Noah. Can't tell yet if it was an accident or intentional." She swung her gaze toward me on the last word.

Clearly it was only me she was stonewalling. I wanted to say *give me a break*, but I bit down on my lip instead. This was taking the whole "everyone who hasn't lived here for at least ten years is an outsider" thing a bit too far. I couldn't think of any other reason she'd be so certain I'd had something to do with Noah's condition. I'd called it in after all, *and* I'd waited around for help to arrive.

"I found him unconscious in Key's stall." I may have emphasized *found him* a little more than was absolutely necessary. At least I had the self-restraint not to glare at the woman who thought I'd actually harm someone on purpose.

Elise swiveled her gaze back to me. "You might not want Russ present for the rest of our chat."

I started to cross my arms over my chest, then remembered one hand was still partly covered in Noah's blood. That thought took some of the fight out of me and the snarky answer fizzled out before hitting my lips. "I'm fine with Russ being here."

Russ might know more about who would want to hurt Noah or how Noah might have gotten himself injured than I did anyway, and if she sent him away, she wouldn't get the information she needed to solve this.

She shrugged in a don't-say-I-didn't-warn-you way. "Based on your reputation, I have to ask. What was the nature of your relationship with Noah?"

Based on my reputation? The only reputation I knew of was one for running my car into things I shouldn't. That wouldn't exactly affect this situation unless she thought I'd run Noah down and dragged his body to the stable. "He's my employee, so I'm not the best one to ask if you want to know about his personal life."

I glanced at Russ with what I hoped was a look that said *jump in anytime*. He was either oblivious or he didn't want to share what he knew about Noah. Or maybe there really wasn't anything to say and I was making assumptions. With all I'd been involved in lately, I'd become even more paranoid than usual. Probably something I should bring up to my counselor in our next session.

"I was talking about your *personal* relationship with Noah," Elise said.

Oohhh. She was implying... I'd never even thought about Noah that way. He was close to fifteen years older than me and, other than Sugarwood, we had nothing in common as far as I knew. If I had committed a crime, it certainly wouldn't have been a crime of passion.

"Nicole and Noah weren't like that," Russ said before I could.

Elise's eyebrows crept up toward her hairline. "I'd like to hear it from her because the rumors around town say different."

I highly doubted the gossip mill was saying anything of the sort. Noah and I had never gone anywhere together unless you counted the hardware store, and the only time I interacted with him at Sugarwood was when he was teaching me how to drive the sleigh and care for the horses or when something needed repairing. Which meant she was likely shaking the tree to see if any fruit fell out.

She was going to go hungry. "I'm not sure where the rumors are coming from, but it's strictly professional."

Her eyebrows flat-lined, like she'd expected me to deny it but was disappointed nonetheless. "Then do you have any guesses as to how this might have happened?"

As an interrogator, she was green. It felt like she'd gotten most of her techniques from a TV cop show rather than from experience in the field. She didn't look young enough for this to be her first investigation, but then again, Fair Haven had a reputation as a sleepy little tourist town. It wasn't until the previous police chief left his position that we found out how much he'd been glossing over and covering up, allowing crime to run unchecked as long as it stayed hidden. I was sure there was even more going on than we knew.

Despite her amateur interview skills, I did need to answer her questions as best I could. My gut said someone had hurt Noah, but I hadn't had a chance to figure out yet *why* I felt that way. That suspicion didn't help with answering the *how* either. I could be wrong.

"I don't know how this happened," I said. "But Noah had more safety rules for dealing with the horses than he did for dealing with the machinery."

And still Russ said nothing. I waited for Elise to ask him a direct question.

Another police car rolled up and more officers I only vaguely recognized climbed out and headed for the stable, presumably to tape off the scene and collect evidence.

Elise tugged on the cuffs of her gloves. "We'll have more questions once the doctor makes his report on the nature of Noah's injuries. Make sure you're available."

She strode back into the stable. What the heck? Had that been her version of *don't leave town*? It definitely felt like a personal vendetta now. We'd never even officially met before and I didn't think I had a guilty-looking face.

Russ laid a hand on my shoulder. "Come on. I'll drive us to the hospital."

I followed him back along the path toward the modern sugar shack. Noah's blood on my hand was dried now, which was almost worse. My skin felt tight and itchy. My fingers tensed with the conflicting desires to scrape it off with my nails and to not touch it. At least this time I wasn't going into shock the way I had when I'd run my car into a person during a snow storm. I was either getting stronger or desensitized. Maybe you couldn't be one without the other.

I strapped myself in. Elise's attitude and words replayed in my mind. For all my professional and dating failures, one thing I'd never struggled with was making friends. People tended to like me, and I'd come to take it for granted. Elise clearly didn't like me, and it felt like it was about more than that I'd been the one to find Noah. I could say the same about Fair Haven in general, though. I'd struggled to make many real connections.

I scrubbed a thumb over my knuckles. "Is Elise always like that?"

It felt weird calling her by her first name, but I'd forgotten to look at her name tag, and she'd skipped the introductions.

Russ shrugged. "Sometimes. She's got well-behaved kids."

For a moment I debated whether thunking my head against the window would be more productive than trying to wring information out of Russel Dantry. Since showing up with a giant bruise on my forehead would only fan the suspicion surrounding my discovery of Noah, I opted for stuffing my hands into the pockets of my coat and letting the topic of Elise drop. What she thought of me wasn't really important. Once the matter moved up the chain to Erik, he'd make sure the investigation went in a more production direction.

In the meantime, we needed to figure out what information might help the police the most. "Do you think Key could have done this to Noah?"

"I didn't see Noah, so I can't really say."

That was a good point. I hadn't considered before how Noah had been positioned, but he'd been lying face up, and the wound that seemed to be bleeding so profusely had been on the back of his head. Key could have knocked him down, but it seemed like he couldn't have delivered the actual wound. Maybe that was why my instincts insisted this wasn't an accident.

That, and he shouldn't have been in Key's stall and in a position to be knocked down at all.

One of the first rules Noah taught me about working with the horses was that I should never handle them loose in the stall. Even though our horses were extremely gentle, if they spooked, they could crush me without meaning to. I was supposed to bring them out and do what he called cross-tying them. Each side of the aisle had a rope attached to the wall, with a clip on the other end that attached to the rings on each side of the horse's halter. It kept them quiet and steady for grooming, caring for their hooves, or putting on their tack to pull the sleigh.

So Noah shouldn't have been in Key's stall in a position to be knocked down hard enough to smash his head open.

The seatbelt suddenly felt like it was cutting into my flesh. I took my hands from my pockets and pulled the belt away from me.

Noah was either negligent or someone had attacked him after all. A suspicion of either could have caused Russ' anxious response to Noah going AWOL. "Is there anyone who might have a reason to hurt Noah? Or did you have a reason to think he might have done something to get himself hurt?"

"Nicole." Russ' voice took on a warning tone, not unlike a parent who wanted their child to stop pushing for something.

Normally I enjoyed Russ playing the role of surrogate uncle, but not today. Today I wasn't his "niece," nor was I poking my nose in where it didn't belong. I was his partner, Noah was my employee, and I'd been the one sitting in a puddle of his blood. Not to mention Elise thought I'd had something to do with it. I needed to know how much or how little I could actually trust Noah with in the future...assuming he survived.

I also needed to know if someone dangerous might have come onto our property.

The thought alone brought goosebumps down my arms. After what happened less than two months ago in our bush, I already didn't feel safe walking the grounds alone anymore. It'd only been in the last week or so that I'd felt secure enough to go back and forth in the daylight without always taking the dogs or another person with me.

"If you have a suspicion about why this happened, I deserve to know about it. Sugarwood is as much mine as it is yours."

Russ' shoulders still rode high, stiff and unnaturally close to his ears. It made him look like he had even less of a neck than usual. "You knowing won't help anything."

"That's not the point."

The words came out snippier than I intended. I smoothed my clean palm over my jeans and kept the dirty hand clenched beside me. Getting frustrated with Russ wouldn't make him talk. And from past experience, I knew that if I pushed him for information without giving him a solid reason to share, he'd lock down tighter than a high-security vault. Maybe I could at least convince him to share what he knew with the authorities.

"I understand that you don't want to spread gossip. That's not what I'm asking you to do. If Noah's in some sort of trouble, you need to tell the police. They can't help him otherwise. And if he did this to himself by accident, it's not right to let the police waste resources investigating something that wasn't a crime."

Russ' shoulders dropped a fraction. "They wouldn't be able to help him even if I told them. Besides, if this turns out to have been an accident, Noah doesn't need all of Fair Haven PD knowing his private business."

I wasn't sure if we were making progress or talking in circles. Russ had basically admitted that there might be someone who would want to hurt Noah, but he refused to say who, to either me or the police.

The police in their interrogations and lawyers in the courtroom often used questions that didn't give the respondent a means of escape. Either answer implicated them. I didn't want to be that person anymore. I didn't want to use those tactics. But I also didn't trust Russ to know when something needed to be shared and when it didn't. He'd proven his willingness to prioritize discretion over common sense more than once in the past. If I didn't push this, and someone else was hurt, either by the person who hurt Noah or by Noah himself, I'd be partly responsible for it. I'd been down that road before, and I had no intention of going back.

I shifted to face him. "I either need to be certain someone else hurt Noah or we need to talk about firing him. If this was negligence, next time someone innocent might be hurt. That'd be on us because we let loyalty to Noah blind us to the risk."

Russ stopped the truck in the hospital parking lot and turned off the engine. "I don't think it was negligence. Poor choices and bad judgment maybe, but not negligence."

I crossed my arms, trying not to flinch as the hand with the dried blood touched my side. If I'd been standing, I would have planted my hands on my hips instead in an imitation of my mom's *don't mess with me* stance.

Russ reached for the door handle.

I hit the lock button on the dash below the radio. "We're not going in until you explain."

Oh dear Lord, I sounded like my mother. I opened my mouth to apologize and take it back when Russ drooped in his seat.

"You're right," he said. "I never would've held this back from your uncle."

My Uncle Stan had been one of the best men I'd ever known. Living up to him was something I might never be able to do. It was understandable that Russ would struggle with the transition. He and Uncle Stan worked side by side for ten years before Uncle Stan passed away, and then I came in, a thirty-year-old with no knowledge of maple syrup except that I liked it on pancakes and French toast. No wonder he saw me as the junior partner even though I controlled the majority interest in the business.

Russ sucked in a big breath of air that sounded almost like a whale shooting water out its blowhole. "Noah has a little problem. An addiction."

*A little problem* and *addiction* weren't analogous terms in my mind, but it didn't surprise me that Russ wanted to downplay it even now. So many questions burst into my mind that I could barely isolate one to ask.

The most logical place to start seemed to be with what type of addiction Noah had. Porn wouldn't have ended up with him bleeding in a horse stall. It could be a substance. Fair Haven's dark side surely had a way for people to obtain drugs, and between Beaver's Tail Brewery and the local bars, alcohol wasn't hard to come by. But I hadn't seen signs of either on Noah. No smell of alcohol or marijuana. No bloodshot eyes. No trouble showing up on time and completing tasks. Until today, he'd been our most reliable employee.

Then again, at this point Russ still managed the employees the same way he had while Uncle Stan was alive. Even though I was trying to learn all aspects of the business, I'd spent most of my time over the past six weeks on paperwork and other administrative tasks.

"Do you think he was high or drunk, and that's why he wasn't careful around the horses?" I asked.

Russ shook his head so hard that, on a man with a narrower neck, I'd have worried about him snapping something. "Naw. Nothing like that. Noah was...is a gambler."

The past tense grated along my ears. "He's not gone yet. It might not have been as bad as it looked."

Russ's caterpillar-like eyebrows drew together. "I didn't mean it that way. Your uncle told me that an addict's always an addict. The only difference is whether the addiction's in remission like a cancer or actively killing them."

I'd heard him say the same thing. Uncle Stan never let people say he *was* an alcoholic because he saw himself as an ongoing alcoholic who'd been sober for a certain length of time. Seeing his struggle first-hand was why I didn't drink even socially. "Was Noah in remission?"

His jowly face drooped, reminding me once again of a sad bulldog. "I thought so until today."

# Chapter 3

My lungs felt like they didn't have enough space to hold the air I needed. "You think someone hurt Noah because he owed them money?"

Russ rubbed both hands over his head, making his hair even more mad-scientist than it was before. "Noah's been attending meetings, but it wouldn't be the first time he slipped. And every time he does, he ends up owing more. He worked at Quantum Mechanics before coming to Sugarwood, and he got himself fired from that job for stealing to pay off some of his debts."

What had Uncle Stan been thinking, hiring a gambler with a history of theft? As soon as I asked myself the question, I knew the answer. Uncle Stan had been a struggling addict. His heavy drinking destroyed his heart. He'd have wanted to give Noah a second chance, too.

"Has he slipped since he came to Sugarwood?"

Russ visibly flinched. "Just once. The night the old sugar shack burned down, he found you 'cause he was coming home late from a poker game."

Maybe I shouldn't have demanded Russ tell me. How was I supposed to trust Noah now? I hit the unlock button and climbed out of the truck. "Let's see what the doctor says about his injuries."

This could all have been a horrible accident. It'd still leave us back at negligence, and that prospect wasn't much better. On days like this, I wished life came with a do-over button.

Russ and I entered the hospital, and while he asked after Noah at the desk, I ducked into the nearest bathroom and washed Noah's blood off my hand. I scrubbed long after all the traces of red were gone, but I could still feel it there.

When I came out, Russ waved me over. "The nurse says they can't tell us anything about Noah's condition since we aren't family, but I gave her the name of his cousin. Once Oliver gets here, I'm sure he'll fill us in."

*Oliver* wasn't a name I recognized, so I wasn't counting on anything on my behalf, but Russ seemed to have a connection to nearly everyone in the town. I swear, if the man had run for mayor, he would have won.

I slouched down in one of the hard plastic waiting room chairs, and Russ took the one next to me.

Instead of leaning back, he perched on the edge. He swallowed hard, making his Adam's apple bob, opened his mouth, and snapped it shut again.

I sat straight up in my seat. He looked like he wanted to say something more, and that I'd like it even less than what he'd already told me.

I hated suspense. Once I had all the facts, I could make plans and develop strategies. I could be proactive.

Uncertainty made me want to scale a rock cliff with my bare hands. "What is it?"

Russ avoided making eye contact. "I think we should call Mark."

The muscles in my stomach spasmed like I'd done too many sit-ups. For over a month now, I hadn't had any contact with Mark beyond a cordial nod when we saw each other at church. And every smile I had to fake when I saw him or heard him mentioned still hurt like I'd slammed my hand into a lit burner on the stove. If I was ever going to stop wishing circumstances had been different, that he wasn't married, I couldn't have anything to do with him. Hadn't we just been talking about addictions? Mark was mine, and one sip could not only knock me off the wagon but drag me behind it as well.

Russ held up his hand in a *wait, wait* gesture. "He's the county medical examiner. He's seen more intentional injuries than any doctor here, and he'll know better than whatever ER doctor Noah gets whether someone could have done this to him or if it was accidental."

Part of me wanted to plant my hands over my ears and hum like a petulant child. Russ' explanation made complete sense, and if the county medical examiner were anyone but Mark, I might have even thought to suggest it myself.

Russ glanced to his left and then past me, as if making sure no one was within hearing distance. He leaned toward me. "Look, Nikki, whatever happened between you two, it isn't worth staying upset over this long. I've lost enough people I loved to know that much at least. I've got to live the rest of my life with the regrets I have over your Uncle Stan and me being on the outs when he died. You and Mark..." He shook his head. "It's been years since I'd seen him as happy as he was since you came around."

Ripples of guilt swirled around inside me. For hurting Mark. For not confiding in Russ. But my decision to end my friendship with Mark before it turned into an adulterous relationship had been the right one. I wasn't going back on it.

I could at least explain the truth to Russ and then he'd drop the matter. I hadn't wanted to initially because I was afraid it would remind him of mistakes he'd made in the past. Perhaps I should have told him because he, of all people, would understand my decision.

Both of us were trying very hard not to repeat our past mistakes.

"Mark didn't do anything wrong. I just—"

Russ jumped to his feet. "There's Oliver. I'll be right back."

He waddled over to a man who'd entered the ER waiting room.

I picked at my thumbnail, a habit my mom had always found unladylike and my dad called a sign of weakness. It figured that, when I finally got up the courage to admit why I'd broken off my seemingly innocent friendship with Mark, we'd be interrupted.

Russ led the man back over to where I waited. I got to my feet.

"Nicole, this is Oliver Miller, Noah's cousin."

I rubbed at my eyes to make sure I wasn't mistaken. Oliver Miller was Owl Man, the dispatcher who'd been on duty at the police station the night I hit a body in a snowstorm. He wore the same large round glasses and wide-eyed expression he had then, but instead of the uniform that I'd mistakenly thought was a police uniform at the time, he now wore the classic grease-stained powder-blue coveralls of Quantum Mechanics. He looked close to Noah in age.

Oliver absently shook my hand. I couldn't be sure if he recognized me or not, but I couldn't blame him for being distracted.

"Do we know what room Noah will be in yet?" he asked.

"I'll go with you to the desk to ask," Russ said.

Russ clapped a hand on his shoulder. It looked a little awkward with the height difference between them—Russ was closer to my height than he was to Oliver's—but Oliver seemed to appreciate it.

He gave Russ a weak smile. "Thanks."

They headed for the check-in desk, and I tucked my hands between my knees. Maybe it was all the talk of Mark, or maybe it was seeing how worried Oliver was over Noah, but I suddenly felt that hollowed-out sensation in the pit of my stomach. The only family I had in the world were my parents out in Washington, DC. One day they'd be gone, and then there'd be no one to come rushing to the hospital if anything happened to me. My best friend Ahanti was like a sister, but even she was in Virginia and soon to be married. It's not like she'd always be able to drop everything and fly halfway across the country.

My life was definitely not the way I'd imagined it would be by the time I was thirty.

I gave myself a mental shake. I might not have everything I wanted, but I loved Sugarwood, and I was finally figuring out what I really wanted from life. That had to count for something.

Russ and Oliver were gone for nearly forty-five minutes before I spotted Russ heading back in my direction.

Once he got closer, Russ waved for me to join him. "The doctor's ready to talk to Oliver, and Oliver's good with us coming along."

We met Oliver at the elevator and rode up two floors. A small headache blossomed in a line above my eyebrows as we rode, and I massaged my fingers into the space. Logically, I knew that all the terrible things that had happened in Fair Haven since I'd first arrived weren't my fault, but on a less rational level, I couldn't help feeling a bit like a harbinger of doom. Noah only added to the body count.

The doctor waited outside the door of Noah's room. I peered inside while Oliver gave his consent for the doctor to explain Noah's condition with Russ and me present. Wires trailed off of Noah like tentacles, and a white bandage covered his head.

The doctor rubbed his chapped red hands together like constant washing had turned it into a tic. "Noah's head wound caused some fluid to build up around his brain. We relieved the pressure, but we can't know yet what permanent damage might have been done or if he'll regain consciousness."

I looked back into Noah's room again. I couldn't quite make the words sink in. He looked peaceful, like he was sleeping. The idea that he might not ever wake up didn't seem real.

Oliver lifted his glasses and rubbed a hand over his eyes. "I need a minute," he said.

He moved down the hallway instead of into Noah's room, putting plenty of space between himself and us.

I exchanged a glance with Russ and nudged my chin forward. With Oliver out of earshot, now was a good time to ask the doctor about the nature of Noah's injuries. If they seemed perfectly normal, then we'd have avoided upsetting Oliver more by suggesting anything otherwise. And I could rest easier that Elise wouldn't be knocking on my door later, wanting to continue our interview.

Russ jiggled the keys in his pocket. "Were you able to tell what caused Noah's injuries?"

"Injury, singular." The doctor looked back over his shoulder at where Oliver had gone as if he wasn't sure whether or not his permission to speak in front of us extended to sharing information he hadn't already told the family. "He had one blow to the back of the head. The EMTs who brought him in said he was found in a horse stall, so the most probable cause is that he was kicked or knocked down and he hit his head on something."

If he'd been kicked, shouldn't he have had at least two wounds, one from the initial blow and a second when his head hit the ground?

I wasn't a doctor—that was probably the one thing I would have been worse at than being a lawyer, since squeamish didn't begin to describe my reaction to things being outside that belonged inside. But as a lawyer, I knew a logical fallacy when I heard one.

Growing up with my parents, I could identify fallacious arguments before I could multiply. Noah's doctor was assuming correlation proved causation. Just because Noah was found in a horse stall didn't necessarily mean the horse had contributed to his injuries. The nature of the injuries themselves should lead to the determination of what had caused them.

"Did the shape and size of the wound support that?" I asked. "Or could something else have caused his head wound?"

The doctor looked down at me over the top of his glasses, the crinkles in his forehead forming three wavy horizontal lines. "There's no need to unnecessarily complicate this by coming up with wild theories. The simplest solution is usually the right one."

My mother's firm voice played in my head. *As a woman, you'll always have to fight harder to be taken seriously.*

But maybe it wasn't a woman thing. Maybe it was a young person thing or a you're-not-a-doctor thing. Or maybe the man simply had a sizeable ego and didn't like to be questioned. I didn't want to make it about gender if it wasn't.

Unfortunately, any of those reasons left me blockaded, and I didn't have a good way to signal Russ to push the matter. He'd have needed more than a firm look to convince him to do anything. The man wasn't just reluctant to rock the boat. He was afraid to even ripple the water.

"Now," the doctor pursed his lips, "if you'll excuse me, I need to discuss options and outcomes with the actual family."

He strode down the hall to where Oliver was despite Oliver's request for some time alone. I almost went after him to distract him longer, but the expression on Russ' face stopped me.

His bottom lip hung down and his furry eyebrows slanted in, forming a valley of disbelief between his eyes. "He sounds like he's guessing about the cause of Noah's injury."

I could almost hear him thinking *this is why we should have called Mark.* I chewed on the inside of my cheek. Maybe I was being selfish and childish. It wasn't like Mark coming to check on Noah would mean we had to renew our friendship. We could meet in a professional capacity, civil without being friendly. And if the doctor wasn't going to actually investigate the cause of Noah's injury, then what other choice did we have? Noah's injuries might be accidental. In that case, we should focus on getting him better and worry about why it happened and making sure it didn't happen again once he was healed.

But if someone had attacked him, the police needed to know. That person might come back to finish the job once they found out Noah had survived.

I swallowed to moisten my suddenly dry mouth. "I think it's time to call Mark."

# Chapter 4

I let Russ make the call so that it wouldn't seem to come from me. Mark didn't argue or question when Russ told him what had happened and what we wanted. Russ said he needed help, and Mark came.

As hard as I tried, I couldn't stop the twist in my heart. His wife was a lucky woman to have a husband she could always count on to be there for her, assuming, of course, that he treated her the same way he treated all the other people in his life.

Oliver went in to sit by Noah's bed, and Russ and I headed down the hallway to wait by the elevators. When Mark stepped off, he nodded at me briefly, the same way he had the few times we'd run into each other since our talk about how we needed to end our friendship. It was a nod that said *I don't want to be rude by not acknowledging you exist.* It was also a nod that didn't encourage any more interaction than that.

I tried not to let it hurt me. I had no right for it to hurt. The decision to end our friendship had been mine, not his.

He turned toward Russ. "Do you know who Noah's doctor is?"

"Dr. Johnson," Russ said. "He's the doctor who saw him in the ER. Noah doesn't have a regular doctor as far as I know."

Mark's lips thinned. "I was hoping for Santos. We'll have to come at it differently now." He rubbed his thumb over his bottom lip. "I can take a look at Noah unofficially, but unless Johnson's willing to sign off on it as suspicious, I don't have any authority here. The best I might be able to do is ask him as a professional courtesy to run a few additional tests. Is Oliver here yet?"

Russ nodded, and I marveled once again at the way everyone in this town seemed to know everyone else. They'd lived their lives together, and that built a sense of connectedness. As much as I fought against it, I was the wrong-colored crayon.

"Since he's official next of kin, it'd help if we had him on our side," Mark said.

Russ led the way down the hall, with Mark next to him. Even though it went against all my natural tendencies, I hung back and tried to stay on the sidelines. My parents had raised me to take charge and be noticed. Stepping aside felt about as comfortable as chewing an ice cube. But I wasn't the one who could do the most good here.

When we entered Noah's room, Oliver was sitting by his side, staring.

Something flickered across Mark's face, like a mixed-up bowl of regret, sympathy, and sadness. It felt like all those times before where I'd suspected he had one foot in the present and the other was caught on something in the past. Now that I wasn't his friend anymore, I'd probably never know the cause. That didn't stop me from wanting to smooth the lines out of his forehead and tease him until he flashed his dimples.

Mark pulled a chair from the other side of the room over to where Oliver sat. "Russ and Nicole asked me to come. They thought you might like someone to talk to who'd be able to give you a second opinion and make sure that every option for Noah's recovery has been explored."

Oliver blinked in my direction. His blinks always seemed to take a fraction of a second longer than a normal person's. That might be part of why he reminded me so much of an owl.

"That was nice of them," he said. "But the doctor said he got knocked down or kicked by those horses. Don't know what kind of a second opinion we need on that."

Mark crossed an ankle over his knee. "Well, I'd like to rule out a different cause for Noah's fall, like a stroke or a seizure. I'd have also recommended a check of his blood sugar levels if your family has a history of type 2 diabetes. We can't tell any of that unless we run some tests, and treatment will vary depending on the cause of his fall."

Mark sounded so self-assured. If he hadn't told me that he struggled with social interactions, I never would have guessed. He'd learned to hide it well. A twinge of regret twisted my heart, but not for the loss of Mark's friendship this time.

As hard as I'd tried, I'd never learned how to hide my nerves when speaking in a courtroom. That failing had doomed my career as a lawyer and ensured my parents would never be proud of me. I'd had to accept that when I gave up practicing law to move to Fair Haven, but it still ached sometimes, like phantom pains in an amputated limb.

Oliver's eyes had gone even rounder than before, a condition I wouldn't have thought possible. He swore. "I didn't realize so many other things could have gotten him here."

Mark was nodding. "And you and I both know from working with the police that we need to at least consider that someone did this *to* Noah."

Oliver cursed again, but it had a different quality this time. More like he was cursing at Mark for suggesting it. "Noah's been working hard to turn things around. We both have. Neither of us wanted to end up like our drunk, worthless dads. There's no one anymore who'd want to hurt him."

The *anymore* was telling. At some point, there had been someone who wanted to hurt him.

I tapped my fingers against my leg. Noah's occasional slips back into his addictive patterns meant that even though he was trying to change the course of his life, he might have still made enemies—including people he owed money to.

But it looked like following that path in the conversation would only turn Oliver against us. He was determined to defend Noah's character, something that seemed common among the people who'd lived their whole lives in Fair Haven. If they ever accepted me fully as one of their own, I'd have the staunchest defenders I could ask for. In the meantime, I wore a scarlet O, for outsider.

Where Oliver was concerned, we needed to approach this from a different angle. In an interview-type situation, Mark tended to run straight at a problem, so it was time for me to move from the sidelines, literally and figuratively.

I stepped to the end of Noah's bed. If there was one thing I'd learned from my time as a defense attorney, it was that being a victim of a crime didn't necessarily mean you'd done anything wrong. "Good people, innocent people, are attacked all the time. For all we know, someone went into the stable looking for things to steal and Noah caught them."

Mark slid a look in my direction, eyes crinkled at the corners, that said *good point*, and for a second, it felt like it had when we'd worked together to solve Uncle Stan's murder.

Oliver followed the look and gave his uncanny blink. "I hadn't thought about that."

Mark rose to his feet. "So what I'd like to do is go talk to Dr. Johnson, with your permission, and see what other tests we could run to rule out the possibilities."

Oliver nodded. Russ told Oliver we'd check in with him later to see how Noah was doing, and we filed out. The hallway felt wide open in comparison to the cramped room.

Mark motioned us down the hallway a bit. "I should be able to get a look at the shape and dimension of the wound as well. That'll help us figure out what might have made it. Hopefully with all of the extra testing, we'll know better whether this was an accident or not. I'll let you know the results."

I met Mark's gaze for the first time since he'd arrived. I could take comfort from the fact that it contained no malice at least. He'd forgiven me.

"Thank you," I said. "For helping us. Helping Noah."

"Any time."

And the soft tone of his voice made me think he meant it.

# Chapter 5

It was a good thing I'd always been an early riser because apparently feeding and cleaning the horses was the first thing Noah normally did every day. With him gone, those tasks had fallen to me.

Russ and I considered doing three rounds of rock-paper-scissors to see who'd end up with the job, but when we stopped to think for a moment, we realized that I had the knowledge and skillset to muck a stall but not to troubleshoot the things that might come up with the maple syrup production. If only my mom could see me now, she might actually admire my determination to keep my business running.

On second thought, this was one of those times when I was thankful she couldn't see me. Or smell me.

I tossed the last forkful into the wheelbarrow and rolled it out of the stall, past where I'd cross-tied Key. Cleaning his stall had taken nearly twice as long as cleaning Leaf's stall because I'd had to scrape out all the shavings matted together with Noah's blood. Which for me meant stopping regularly for fresh air whenever my stomach got queasy over the thought of exactly what I was doing.

As I moved past, he snuffled my hair, his breath warm and moist. He'd been lackluster today, almost as if he knew something were wrong. Maybe he did. I'd never had a pet before adopting my dogs, but they seemed to have a sixth sense about when I was having a bad day.

Yesterday certainly counted as a bad day, which probably explained why I'd been tripping over a dog every time I turned around last night. They refused to leave me alone.

I'd just dumped the wheelbarrow outside for the final time when my cell phone rang in my pocket. I stripped off my heavy gloves and fished it out.

Mark.

My stomach dropped like an elevator plunge. It felt like years since I'd seen his name on my phone and also like it'd been yesterday. For a single ring, I let myself pretend that everything was right between us and that he was calling just to chat.

Unfortunately, my logical side stomped down on the fantasy much too quickly. He was more likely calling with news about Noah.

I tapped the screen to take the call.

"Sorry to bother you," he said. "I tried calling Russ, but he didn't answer."

Mark's voice had a hesitant tone to it that I'd never heard before. Almost like he was afraid I'd be angry at him for calling me. I swallowed hard, but the tightness in my throat fought back.

I'd spare him from any attempts to make small talk at least. "No problem. I'm guessing you have news."

We sounded like acquaintances. It was what I'd wanted, but it felt about as good as accidentally slamming my big toe into a rock.

"Yeah," Mark said. "I need you to check something for me in the stall where you found Noah."

I propped the phone between my shoulder and ear, leaned the wheelbarrow against the stable wall, and took my phone back into my hand. If this conversation lasted long, I'd need to swap hands. My fingers were already chapping red.

"Does this mean Noah's tests came back negative?"

"For everything." He kept his voice low, which made me think he might be still at the hospital and didn't want anyone to overhear. "The wound on the back of his head was crescent shaped, almost like a horseshoe, but unless your horses shrunk from the last time I saw them, the wound's not from one of them. It's a fraction of the size of a normal horse's hoof, let alone a Clydesdale's."

I paused next to Key and stroked a hand down his cheek. He sighed and drooped his head down into my touch. It was almost like he understood he'd been acquitted.

But should I feel relieved about that or more upset? On one hand, it meant Noah hadn't brought this on himself accidentally. On the other hand, it meant he'd made someone angry enough that they put him in a coma.

Except Mark still wanted me to look in Key's stall, and he hadn't said anything about calling Erik to turn this into an open investigation.

"I'm guessing Dr. Johnson doesn't want to sign off on Noah's injury as suspicious?"

"He's convinced the wound was made by something in the stall when Noah fell. If I'd already been brought in on this case, I could overrule anyone, even the sheriff. As it is, it'd be nice if I had something more concrete before I took it to Erik."

Having Erik Higgins as the interim police chief should mean we had a better chance of being taken seriously, but Erik was also more by-the-book than the man who wrote the book. Since they'd never declared the stable a crime scene, nothing in it could be used as official evidence in a trial. Hopefully, though, if we could show him that there wasn't anything in the stall that could have made a wound like Noah's, he'd consider investigating this as an attempted murder.

I ducked under Key's neck and went into his stall. "So I'm looking for something horseshoe shaped. Does it need to be near where I found Noah?"

"Look the whole stall over, just in case."

We stabled Key and Leaf in oversized box stalls, eleven feet by eleven feet. The back walls were completely smooth because they doubled as the back wall of the stable itself. The other three sides were smooth wood on the bottom and vertical bars on the top, with an opening over the door for us to throw in hay and the horses to stick their heads out and a "window" that we could open and close in order to fill the water bucket and feed trough that hung on the front wall of the stall.

The only place Noah could have possibly hit his head was on the feed trough or water bucket hook, but those were on the other side of the door from where I'd found him. But because Mark asked me to, I'd check them anyway.

The feed trough was black rubber, with no round protrusions and no blood smears. The heated bucket did have a horse-shoe shaped part on its handle where it hooked to the stall.

"How big was the wound?" I asked.

"No bigger than your palm. Do you see something?"

I held my palm up to the bucket handle. Conceivably it could be around the right size, but the metal was clean. With how much Noah's head wound had bled, it should have left some spatter.

And the bucket was at my chest height. Even if Key knocked Noah backward and he hit his head as he fell, I wasn't sure he could have smashed his head hard enough on the protruding loop of the handle to knock himself unconscious. Plus, he'd still have been on the wrong side of the stall.

"Nicole?"

Right. Mark was waiting for me to tell him what I found.

"I see something that's a possibility, but the placement makes it unlikely."

Silence stretched on the line.

"This would be easier if I could take a look," Mark finally said.

And there was the crux of it. He'd called Russ first. He'd tried to have me simply take a look. But in the end, we weren't going to get anywhere if Mark didn't come to Sugarwood, where I was, and look. I was only guessing as to whether something in Key's stall could fit. Mark had been the one to see the wound.

I glanced down at myself. I'd put on my most ragged clothes and one of Uncle Stan's old coats. That, coupled with the fact that I smelled like manure and other animal byproducts, should make it safe to be around Mark.

"I have Key out of his stall right now if you want to come."

"I'll be there in about five minutes. It shouldn't take me long to look the stall over."

We ended the call and I grabbed up one of the brushes. The more dirt and fur—was it fur on horses or hair?—I could get on myself before Mark showed up, the better. I worked my way down Key's legs since I didn't want to drag out the footstool I needed to groom their backs and necks.

When I reached his left front, dark brown flecks clung to the white hairs of his sock. I pulled the brush away and leaned in closer.

My gut reaction was that it was blood. If it were blood, that might lend weight to Dr. Johnson's belief that this had been an accident. How else would Key have ended up with blood on his foreleg?

The more probable explanation, though, was that it was mud or manure. Mark had said the wound was much too small to have come from a kick by Key.

"No dogs today?" Mark's voice asked from the doorway.

It was a good thing Key's leg blocked my face or I'm sure Mark would have seen how being around him affected me. Even though I'd seen him only yesterday, it felt like too long. When I was back in Virginia, packing up my life, we hadn't gone a day without talking, texting, or emailing. It'd been almost like he died in the past weeks.

I straightened and tossed the brush back into the plastic container where we kept the brushes and hoof picks. "Velma hasn't learned not to walk under the horses' bellies yet, and I don't want her to get stepped on, so I left them at home." I rolled my eyes. "With everything else that's going wrong this month already, I don't need a dog with a broken leg on top of it."

Mark's dimple popped out, and we stood awkwardly staring at each other. Small talk wasn't his strength, and I didn't trust myself to make any.

I motioned toward the stall. "Feel free to poke around."

Mark nodded and moved past Key and out of sight. I leaned my forehead against Key's warm, fuzzy neck. I kept thinking these interactions with Mark would get easier and less awkward. When I called Ahanti for our regular Sunday afternoon chat, she'd suggested I sign up for the online dating site where her sister met her fiancé. I'd brushed off the idea, but maybe I should ask her for more details. Maybe what I needed was to start dating again. Of course, that hadn't worked out well with Erik.

"I don't think it could be from the bucket handle if that's what you were looking at," Mark said from beside me.

I jumped. Key twitched his ears, but otherwise his big body stayed still. How could anyone think he'd knocked down or kicked Noah?

Key pushed his nose into Mark's cheek, and Mark rubbed Key's forehead. "I guess that's his way of thanking me for trying to exonerate him."

A warm bubble wrapped around my heart, and all my common sense couldn't seem to pop it. I tucked my hair behind my ears and looked away. There had to be someone like Mark, but not Mark, out there for me. "Does this mean you're going to call Erik about it?"

Key lipped at Mark's hair. Mark stepped out of his reach. "Yeah. A lot of the situation is still ambiguous, but I think I can make a good case that the angle of the wound should have been different if Noah hit his head on the bucket handle during a fall. He'd have had to hit it with a lot more force too than I think would reasonably happen during a fall. If Key kicked him into the bucket, he should have had a bruise somewhere showing the impact."

It was semi-official then. Noah's injury hadn't been an accident. Someone had come onto Sugarwood's ground and hit him hard enough to put him into a coma.

A chill threaded over me despite my warm clothes, and I crossed my hands around my waist. "Thanks for taking the time to come out and check."

"It's all part of the job." Mark shoved his hands into his pockets and nodded his head toward the stall. "I'll leave you to your work."

After all he'd done, it felt rude to send him off that way. Or maybe my subconscious was trying to find sneaky ways to spend an extra minute or two with him. "Let me at least walk you to your truck."

We left the stable, but instead of Mark's charcoal grey truck, a maroon car sat in the lot. "Did you sell your truck?"

Mark's dimples peeked out. "It's at Quantum Mechanics for the brakes. My sister-in-law loaned me hers so I wouldn't have to sacrifice my nose or ears walking everywhere in the cold."

"The first person to open a car rental shop here will make a fortune."

Mark chuckled. He opened the car door, but didn't climb in. Instead he angled back to face me slightly. "How are things going? With Sugarwood and...everything?"

By *everything*, he probably meant the relationship he thought I had with Erik. Erik and I had gone on a couple of dates during my first couple of weeks in Sugarwood, but it hadn't gone any further than that because Erik figured out I had feelings for Mark. We'd become friends instead and got together every week or two for breakfast at The Burnt Toast.

But when I'd told Mark I couldn't spend time with him anymore, I took the coward's way out and let him assume it had something to do with Erik and me being a couple. Guilt ground like sand between my teeth at the memory. I could clear it up now, but that would mean admitting to the truth. I couldn't spend time with Mark because I was in love with him and he was a married man.

I'd rather clean stalls every day for the rest of my life than admit to that.

"Everything's mostly good," I said. "Our sugar season was off to a rocky start even before Noah, so now we're hoping nothing else goes awry. And you?"

Mark climbed into the car. "Give Russ my best," he said before closing the door.

And I couldn't help but notice that he hadn't answered my question at all.

# Chapter 6

I'd thought I'd hear from Erik sometime that day, telling me that he'd opened an official investigation into what had happened to Noah. But I didn't.

When he still hadn't called me by noon the next day, I was done waiting.

I called his cell phone rather than calling the police station.

"I expected you might call," Erik said in lieu of a hello. "I'd planned to call last night, but we had an accident on Highway 31, just outside town."

I never knew what to say when he told me something like that. The things police officers had to see and cope with on an almost daily basis would have turned me into a jellyfish. But maybe all he needed was for me to listen and let him know that, with all that was happening in the world, I had nothing but respect for the sacrifices law enforcement made to keep everyone else safe.

"I'm sorry," I said. "Were there fatalities?"

"No, thank God." The sound of him rustling papers carried over the line. "I guess you're calling about Noah's case."

"Does that mean it is a case now?"

Erik cleared his throat. "Unfortunately not. Mark made a good argument, but Dr. Johnson lobbied equally as hard that it was accidental."

I understood where he was coming from on having to listen to both sides, and yet I didn't. "But Mark's the expert. You've worked with him for years, and you know he knows what he's talking about."

"I also know that he would say the moon's made of blue cheese if you wanted him to."

A hard, hot ball formed in the pit of my stomach. My first instinct was to defend Mark's integrity. He wouldn't risk convicting an innocent person sometime down the line just to make me happy now.

I pulled the phone away from my face and stuck out my tongue at it to let off some of the pressure. Losing my cool would only prove Erik's point that Mark and I impaired each other's judgment. It might be true in some ways, but not this time. "I'm sorry you think so little of both of us."

Erik sighed. "It's not like that, Nicole. I'm saying this because I'm your friend. I'm both of your friends. And you have to admit it's more likely you're seeing a crime here where there isn't one than that we have another murder in Fair Haven."

Improbable wasn't the same thing as impossible. "I think you're making a mistake if you classify this as an accident."

"Now you sound like Officer Scott."

Officer Scott? Elise? She was the only officer assigned to this case as far as I knew.

"Look," Erik said, his voice quieter than before. "Our whole department is under investigation thanks to the former chief and the things he covered up. Every decision I make right now is questioned and examined for favoritism and corruption because I was his second-in-command. If I don't have a better justification than *Mark examined a patient he had no right to examine because a civilian asked him to*, it won't just be my job. It'll be his and anyone else who's seen as crossing the line with us."

Like Quincey, who'd once let me out of a cell. And the dispatcher who gave me Quincey's cell phone number because I was Stan Dawes' niece. Good men whose only mistake was to help me.

"I understand."

"You know I'd help if I could," he said.

"I know." He always had. He'd become the big brother I'd never had, and I appreciated that he was trying to watch out for his people.

But someone also had to watch out for Noah—one of my people. Whoever had hurt him might come back to finish what they'd started. I couldn't live at the hospital to make sure he was safe, and since the police didn't classify it as a crime, they wouldn't leave him protection either.

If Erik couldn't investigate, I would. I'd find him the evidence he needed to open an official case.

The best lead I had at present was that Noah was a recovering gambler and owed someone money. Finding out the name of Noah's bookie might be enough to give Erik the justification he needed. Hopefully getting the name from Russ wouldn't be like squeezing lemonade from a stone.

I snapped leashes on my dogs and took them with me. They could use the exercise, and Russ had planned to spend today finishing the repairs that we couldn't make yesterday without the parts Noah was supposed to pick up prior to his attack. Thankfully, the temperature had been wrong last night, and the sap wasn't running today. It gave us a little time to catch up.

I swung by the rental shop to grab a pair of snowshoes and a walkie-talkie, then radioed Russ for his location. His voice as he gave it sounded hesitant, but he couldn't exactly ask what I wanted over the radio.

The walk out took us about ten minutes. As soon as we were inside the tree line, I took the leashes off Velma and Toby and let them run free. The first command I'd taught both of them was *come*, and they'd both caught on quickly when they realized a treat waited for them when they did. I wasn't above bribery for good behavior.

I spotted the snowmobile before I saw Russ' barrel-shaped figure weaving through the trees. It wasn't normal for him to take the snowmobile if he was only out this far, but perhaps he had sections to repair all across the bush. Or perhaps the attack on Noah had made him feel his age. I'd called him as soon as Mark left yesterday, and I hadn't heard him sound so defeated since his girlfriend passed away last fall.

Russ raised a hand in greeting. "I have a feeling I'm not going to like whatever brings you out here."

Good news had been in short supply for us lately, but it wasn't like Russ to be so morose. He was usually the level, easy-going one. No high highs, but also no low lows.

Then again, he'd lost Uncle Stan, and now Noah was unconscious in the hospital. If it were me, I'd be wondering what could be coming next. That fear of the future could deflate even the staunchest optimist.

I also couldn't deny that he wasn't going to appreciate what I wanted. "I need the name of Noah's bookie."

His eyebrows came down into a *like heck you do* frown. "I don't know his bookie's name, and even if I did, I wouldn't give it to you."

Russ was one of the world's worst liars. He tended to sweat and twitch when he needed to tell a falsehood. Right now, he looked stern and solid. Which, unfortunately for me, meant he probably *didn't* know the name of Noah's bookie. "Do you have Oliver's phone number?"

Russ had his wagging finger out and his chest puffed up. "There's no reason you need the name of Noah's bookie. You're not the police, and you certainly shouldn't be chasing after whoever hurt Noah. Your luck isn't going to last forever."

Velma bounded through the snow drift next to us and made two laps around us before sliding to a stop and planting her fist-sized paw on top of a branch, pinning it to the ground so she could tug on the other end. She was already larger than most dogs and lean like a deer. Watching her play like this gave me an equal sense of sadness and satisfaction. She and so many others had been spared from having short and brutal lives, but it'd taken the sacrifice of a good man to bring it about.

I'd rather not have to sacrifice the same amount to save Noah. Russ was right. I wasn't a cat. There weren't nine lives waiting for me to burn through, and even if there had been, I'd have already used up at least five of them.

"Trust me, chasing after a criminal is the last thing I want to do." I crossed my heart for emphasis. "But Erik says he doesn't have enough information to open an actual investigation. I thought if I could give him the name of Noah's bookie it might help."

"Oh." Russ' chest deflated like a popped balloon. "Sorry. This is bringing up some rough memories of what happened to your uncle."

That explained his out-of-character behavior. Grief was one of those emotions where you'd think you were doing better and then something small could come along and send you tumbling back. "At least Noah wasn't negligent."

Russ grunted. "Small favors."

He turned away from me and tightened up one of the replaced joints in the sap line. It was his trademark way of trying to end a conversation. He hadn't given me Oliver's phone number, but I could always call him at work. With the way he'd been dressed when he came to the hospital two days ago, he couldn't work anywhere other than Quantum Mechanics.

I called a goodbye to Russ. I'd let him think he'd won this one, and I'd track Oliver down on my own.

I picked up a cell phone signal a few feet from the edge of the bush and dialed the number for Quantum Mechanics. With the amount of time my car had spent there, I knew it by memory. One more visit and Tony should really give me the mechanic version of frequent flyer miles.

I didn't recognize the man's voice that answered. "Oliver's off today for a family emergency. You can leave a message for him when he gets back in if you'd like."

I opted not to leave a message. If he wasn't at work, my guess was he was at the hospital, sitting with Noah. I called the front desk at the hospital and gave them the room number.

A man answered on the second ring.

"Is this Oliver?"

There was a longer hesitation on the line than I expected. "Yeah. Who's this?"

"Nicole Fitzhenry-Dawes." *Always call yourself their employer when you want to form a connection,* my mom used to tell me, *and their boss when you want to give them an order you expect to be obeyed.* In this case I wanted Oliver to feel like I was on Noah's side, advocating for his best interests. "Noah's employer."

"I remember you," Oliver said, but the way he said it made me think he meant he remembered me from more than just our meeting at the hospital a couple of days ago. "Are you calling to see how Noah's doing?"

I flinched. Normally I preferred face-to-face interactions because it was easier to read people, but this time the phone saved me. If Oliver hadn't said something, I might have jumped right into what I wanted from him, so focused on finding who hurt Noah that I forgot to check on how he was healing. If he was healing.

"How is he doing?" I asked so that I didn't have to lie by directly answering his question.

"The doctor says the swelling's come down in his brain. He should be awake but he's—"

His sentence cut off so abruptly that I stopped walking and checked my phone. I still had a signal, so it hadn't been caused on my end.

"Anyway," Oliver said, "thanks for calling."

"Wait." Hopefully he hadn't hung up already. It'd be mortifying if I had to call back because then it'd been clear what my real motive had been for calling. "I've been trying to provide some information for the police that might help them decide if they should classify Noah's case as criminal. Do you know the name of the man he owed money to?"

Phrasing it broadly seemed more tactful and safer. For all I knew, Noah owed money to more than one person.

"Other than Tony you mean?"

I'd almost forgotten that Noah had gotten himself fired from Quantum Mechanics for stealing. "I didn't know he was paying Tony back for what he took."

"Not sure, but I figured that's what was happening since Tony didn't press charges."

That was interesting information but not helpful. I couldn't see Tony attacking Noah for missing a payment, or even a lot of payments. "Tony's not the only one, though?"

"Naw, but he's the only one I know by name. Noah never told me the name of the guy he placed bets with."

I stomped my foot into the snow and Velma's ears perked up into triangles like she was trying to decide if this was a new game. If this were a game, I could go online and find a cheat to get around this roadblock. "Are you okay with me going into Noah's house and looking around for any records he might have kept?"

"Sure," Oliver said. "And could you empty out the fridge for me. If he comes out of this, he's not going to want to go home to his house smelling like spoiled milk and rotten apples."

I settled the dogs in at home and took the path through the woods to where Noah and Russ' cabins sat. Other than the staff at Short Stack, our pancake house, and Dave who worked at the rental shop and ran the zip line in the summer, Sugarwood only had three full-time employees—Noah, Russ, and me. Since Uncle Stan had technically been their landlord—albeit rent-free—before he died, his key rack had neatly labeled spare keys to each of their homes.

I wiggled the key in Noah's lock until it gave, pushed the door open, and hesitated in the doorway. Even though Oliver gave me permission, it felt like a violation of Noah's privacy.

One of the strangest things about dealing with Uncle Stan's affairs after he died was sorting through his private belongings, things he'd never expected anyone else to see. It'd been bearable then because he'd been my family and he wasn't coming back. But with Noah, if he recovered, I'd have to face him every day knowing more about him than an employer should know about their employee.

But if I wanted to help him, I had no other choice.

I took a long stride across the threshold and dragged the door shut behind me. I'd expected the house to smell like grease and dirt and gasoline since Noah was a mechanic. Instead, his house smelled more like hay and spicy aftershave.

I didn't know Noah well enough to know the best place to look for any records, but I did know he was methodical about organizing his tools. He didn't like anyone touching his toolbox, and his workbench had all his tools hung on labeled nails or stored in neatly labeled, clear plastic boxes.

Since he didn't have any reason to hide his records—Russ and Uncle Stan had known about his habit—the most likely place would be in a desk or filing cabinet. I walked through the living room, kitchen, and breakfast nook, but they were almost sterile, like Noah had already sold everything of value that he owned that wasn't essential for survival. No television. No computer. Nothing of value except a small piece of machinery sitting on a towel, presumably something he was fixing for Sugarwood, but it could also be an item he was repairing for someone else to make extra cash.

The only other room downstairs was his bathroom. I highly doubted he kept his record of his debts in there, though in the crime scene photos I saw during my previous career, I'd seen stranger things kept in the bathroom, including a spray paint gun and a hand juicer. I peeked into Noah's bathroom just in case, but the most interesting thing there was the lack of a shower curtain.

The stairs led up to the house's two small bedrooms. The first was completely empty. The second must have been where Noah slept because it at least had a mattress on the floor, neatly made. A small dresser nestled against one of the walls.

I held my spot in the doorway. The dresser seemed like my best option for finding any information about who Noah owed money to. It was also the most likely spot for him to keep his underwear, and as important as this was, I didn't want to be elbow deep in Noah's boxer shorts...or tightie whities. There were some lines that should never be crossed.

I sucked in a deep breath and strode toward the dresser. I'd take a quick look. Given how Noah organized the rest of his life, he probably wasn't the type of man to keep papers in with his underwear anyway. Fingers crossed, he kept anything pertinent in its own drawer.

I pulled the top drawer open enough to see inside. Jackpot. No underwear, only papers and pictures.

Noah had stacked old credit card bills, neatly labeled with the reference numbers banks gave online when you paid, and elastic-banded together by year. Did bookies accept credit card payments for debts? With people being able to accept payment through their cell phones anymore it was certainly possible, and I didn't want to overlook anything.

I unfolded a couple recent bills and scanned the purchases. Other than the grocery store, a 96ers Bar & Grill, and The Burnt Toast Café, the majority of purchases were ones he'd made for Sugarwood that we reimbursed him for. Nothing jumped out at me as a potential cover name for a bookie's business, and there were no charges to a personal name.

I folded the bills back up and stacked them back on his pile. If I had to rifle through his private business, I could at least be respectful of his filing system.

A nine-by-twelve cream-colored envelope lay next to his stacks of bills. I wiggled it out and popped the flap. It wasn't sealed.

I poured the contents out on the dresser top, and photos slid everywhere. Pictures were the last thing I'd been expecting. I stored all my photos digitally anymore, as did most people I knew. I only printed out ones I wanted to frame and display. I certainly didn't print pictures to stuff them in an envelope in a drawer. But maybe Noah had owned some expensive frames that he'd pawned for cash. That wouldn't surprise me.

Either way, pictures wouldn't help me find his bookie. I started to scoop them back up to slide back into the envelope and froze.

Noah smiled at me from the image, sitting on a large fallen log, a backdrop of trees covered in red and orange behind him. And the young woman sitting on his lap looked barely legal age...maybe not even.

She'd tied her blonde hair back in a ponytail, which made her already lean face look narrower, and turquoise teardrop earrings dangled from her ears. She wore that kind of all-hope-no-fear smile that I'd rarely seen on anyone over the age of twenty-five.

They were both fully clothed, though, so it wasn't like the photo alone proved wrongdoing. For all I knew, Noah had once had a younger sister and she'd died so he took down all her photos and stuffed them out of sight. It wouldn't be the strangest thing a grieving person had done.

I flipped to the next picture.

Whoever the girl-woman was, she wasn't his sister. This picture was close, like Noah held the camera at arm's length to take it, and the image was slightly off-center. Despite that, there was no mistaking that the person Noah was passionately kissing was the same girl-woman from the previous photos. The turquoise earrings were the same.

I'd seen enough. I averted my eyes while I shoved the photos back, just in case any of the others weren't so innocent.

A burning sensation grew at the bottom of my throat and spread down into my stomach. I should turn these pictures over to Erik as well. If Noah had been inappropriate with an underage girl, that meant an angry father or uncle or brother could have been the one to hit Noah in the head. Based on what Mark had said about the angle of the wound, it couldn't have been someone shorter than Noah, which ruled out 80 percent of women and the girl herself.

I'd pray she was overage. I hated to think that Noah could have been capable of acting inappropriately toward a minor.

I set the packet on top of the dresser. If the girl-woman in the photo were legal age, I'd still need the bookie's name. Even if she wasn't, the bookie might be the one who hurt Noah anyway. Finding these pictures simply meant the police would have more suspects to investigate.

A few other photos floated around loose in the drawer. Noah with an older woman who looked like his mom. Noah, Russ, and Uncle Stan standing in front of the horses and sleigh. Noah at what looked like a Quantum Mechanics Christmas party with Oliver and Tony. Nothing in any of them suggested anything abnormal or pointed to anyone else who might have wanted Noah dead. In fact, he looked well-liked.

I moved the photos to the side. Underneath was a manila folder. I flipped it open.

It looked like a ledger of payments, like you'd expect to find when someone was paying off a debt. Unfortunately, Noah hadn't written down the name of the person or persons he owed money to.

I continued turning the pages. If Noah hadn't left some trail, I didn't know where to go next. The man took minimalism to a whole new level.

I set aside another page. The one behind it was a photocopy of three checks. I couldn't help but smile. Noah might have been an addict, but he wasn't entirely stupid. He'd covered his tail by copying every check he'd written to repay his bookie so that he'd have proof of what he'd already paid off.

The checks were all written out to a George Abbott. I'd found the name I was looking for.

I squirmed in place on the cold metal bench along the wall of the police station. The man at the front desk, who turned out to be the same one who put me in contact with Officer Quincey Dornbush the last time I'd been tangled up in a murder investigation, had told me Erik was on the phone, but he'd be out as soon as he finished.

The front door to the station swung open, and Elise Scott strode in. I could tell the moment she spotted and recognized me because her step faltered slightly. She changed directions and stopped in front of the desk.

"What's she doing here?" Elise asked the desk clerk.

I think she meant it to be a whisper, but the waiting area was empty except for me. The only noises were the ruffling of the papers the desk clerk had been looking through and the rattle of the furnace pushing not-nearly-warm-enough air out of the vents.

The temptation to answer her myself was almost more than I could handle, but I didn't want to be one of those snarky women. I'd always found that women like that were a lot more fun to read about than they were to know, and I already had enough barriers to break through in Fair Haven without adding a reputation for snarkiness on top of it.

"Nicole?" Erik's voice called from my left.

I glanced up and he waved for me to join him. Once we were both inside his office, he closed the door tightly behind us.

He sank into his chair and nodded toward the one on the other side of the desk. I opted not to sit. I wanted to make it clear that I wasn't butting into this investigation. This was more of an evidence drive-by.

He gave me his characteristic not-quite-a-smile smile. "I'm almost afraid to ask why you're here after our conversation this morning."

I swallowed down an extremely unladylike snort. I couldn't blame him if he was wondering what trouble I'd already managed to get myself in to after we talked this morning. I was probably more familiar with the way to the police chief's office than most of the long-time residents in Fair Haven were. At least this time I could set his mind at ease.

"I got permission from Noah's family to look around his house for anything that might point to who could have wanted to hurt him." I laid the folder and envelope on the desk. "I found the name of the man I think Noah owed money to and some..."

I didn't know how to describe the photos of Noah with the girl-woman. If it turned out she was underage, I'd have to fire him no matter how nice he seemed or how hard a worker he was.

"Some what?" Erik asked.

He hadn't reached for the pile of documents, and the way his lips turned down made me want to squirm. He clearly thought I'd done something outside the lines to get whatever I wanted to show him even though I'd told him how I came by it.

"Some photos I think you should see. They were in his house as well."

He still didn't reach for the documents, and my chest tightened. Didn't he believe me?

Erik rubbed at the shoulder where he'd been shot in January. We'd hoped he wouldn't have any lasting side effects from the wound, but he'd confided in me at our last breakfast that he was still having trouble controlling his aim when he fired his weapon at the range. The doctors said he needed to give it time, but he was starting to be afraid of being confined to desk duty forever, even after the powers-that-be hired a new police chief—a task they seemed to be in no rush to complete.

He must have realized what he was doing because he dropped the hand he'd been massaging his shoulder with to the desk. "I can't look at any of that, and you need to take it with you when you go. Put it back where you found it."

I took a step backward. Of all the things I'd thought he might say, that wasn't on the list. It reminded me too much of how Chief Wilson denied the truth and turned a blind eye to what was happening in Fair Haven. But I also knew Erik wasn't like that, so he must have a good reason. "Why?"

"This isn't an open investigation, and nothing in what you brought proves someone attacked Noah. If I look at it now, and later we do find evidence suggesting Noah was attacked, I won't be able to use it. So put it back in his house, where you found it, and don't mention it to anyone else. I don't even want to know where in the house it was."

I sank down onto the edge of the chair that I'd turned down before. I saw his point, but that left my biggest concern unanswered. "I'm worried that whoever did this won't consider it finished because Noah's still alive. They could smother him in his bed and no one would know until it was too late. Isn't there anything you can do without compromising the department or a future case?"

Erik cracked his knuckles, something I hadn't seen him do before. It must be a sign of the additional stress he was under with the investigation into the department and his questionable recovery on top of running the department. "I can't give him a protective detail as long as it's classified as an accident. I could call the hospital and ask that only people on a list I'll give them be allowed to visit him."

My shoulders slumped. It was something at least, and it should be easy enough for Erik to explain if he was asked. A question had been raised by people close to Noah about whether it was really an accident or not, and he was taking precautions to protect a citizen should this turn out to have been intentional.

It didn't guarantee Noah's safety, though. It was more like a bailing bucket on a boat with a hole. Someone could still sneak past the nurses. They couldn't watch Noah's door every minute, especially given that the patients on the floor far outnumbered the staff. And once someone slipped inside, a staff member would have to actually look in the door to Noah's room to see someone was in there.

And if Noah did recover, he'd be out in the world again, giving whoever attacked him a hundred more opportunities to do it again. This time, they'd probably make sure he was dead before they left.

*Why didn't they make sure he was dead the first time?* the annoying voice of logic in my head whispered.

I didn't have an answer for it, and sitting like a mannequin in Erik's office was only wasting his time and mine.

I rose to my feet, grabbed up the evidence, and turned for the door. Despite the pictures of Noah and the girl-woman, his bookie still seemed the most plausible option for who'd hurt him. If it'd been over money, there was one way to ensure Noah's safety that didn't involve the police.

I'd find his bookie and pay Noah's debt myself.

# Chapter 7

As soon as I was back in my car, I did a search on my phone for George Abbott within the county. Since Noah didn't have a record of missing work, he couldn't have been driving too far away, unless he was simply placing his bets over the phone on horse races or something like that. I doubted he was gambling remotely, though, because Russ did say he'd gone somewhere to gamble the last time he slipped.

Either way, my search for George Abbott came up empty.

I leaned my forehead against the steering wheel. This was so frustrating. All the books featuring private investigators and concerned citizens solving crimes made it sound simple. Gathering any sort of information without the help of the police was definitely harder than they made it seem.

"Stop whining," I said into the middle of my steering wheel. "That's not going to help Noah."

I straightened up and rolled my shoulders. It made sense that a bookie wasn't going to take out a Yellow Pages listing. His business was probably word of mouth, which meant that locals might know where to find him. The problem was, most of the locals I knew well enough to ask weren't going to be inclined to tell me. I couldn't ask Erik, and I knew Russ and Mark wouldn't tell me even if they knew, for fear that I'd do exactly what I planned to do.

The only person I could think of who might know where to find George Abbott and who would be willing to tell me was Oliver. Hopefully he was still at the hospital.

The phone rang six times before anyone picked up.

At the sound of Oliver's voice, I let out the breath I'd been holding. "Sorry to bother you again, but I think I might have figured out who Noah owed money to. Does the name George Abbott sound familiar?"

"Not really, but like I said, Noah didn't tell me who he was gambling with. I think he was trying to protect me from getting caught up like he did. He knew I wanted to be part of the police department, and if I'd gotten into anything like that, it'd be over for me."

There was a hint of bitterness in his voice. He was no longer working at the police station because he made a mistake the night I came in after hitting a body in the road. Even though it wasn't my fault that he'd lost his job, I still felt bad about it. Now wasn't the right time to say how sorry I was, though. If I reminded him of the role I'd unwittingly played, he might not help me out anymore, regardless of the fact that I was trying to protect Noah.

"And you don't know of any Abbotts who live around here?"

A static-filled tap came through the phone, like Oliver bounced a finger off the back of the phone while he thought. "I think the Sports Bar and Grill out on 96 might be owned by an Abbott."

That sounded similar to the charges I'd seen on Noah's credit card bill to a 96ers Bar & Grill. That could be the one Oliver meant.

I thanked him, hung up, and searched for the address. It wasn't far from here, but it was also already the middle of the afternoon, and I should be back at Sugarwood. But if the sap started running again, who knew how long it would be before I could slip away again. It was now or never.

I put the address into my car's GPS and followed its directions out of the police station parking lot.

After the third turn I took, the dark gray car that had been behind me at the first traffic light was still there. The anxious-panicky feeling I sometimes got slithered up from my stomach and into my throat.

Even though I was on my third turn, I'd passed multiple roads and businesses. What were the odds that someone else would be taking this exact route? It was the path to Interstate 96 and the best way to get to Grand Rapids, so it wasn't impossible.

I still couldn't convince the hair on my arms to lie flat, though. It was like I'd rubbed a balloon over my skin.

Pulling into the parking lot of the nearest business and going out the backside would cost me less than a minute, and my GPS would automatically recalculate my route. A slight detour was worth it for peace of mind.

I hit my turn signal and swung into the furniture store parking lot on my right. I wove my way around the building and out the rear exit onto a different street. The dark gray car would continue on its way because they hadn't been following me, they'd lose me even though they had, or I'd know for sure that someone was tailing me.

I stopped at the stop sign at the end of the street and checked my rearview mirror. A dark gray car pulled slowly around the corner of the furniture store.

My hands clenched around the steering wheel, fingernails digging into the material. Crap. Crap, crap, crap.

The odds were way too long to be believed that the dark gray car had gone this way as well by coincidence. I needed to call 9-1-1 or call Erik. Which was the smarter option? Erik would send someone right away, whereas the 9-1-1 dispatcher would probably ask why I thought I was being followed, but calling Erik could put him in a bad spot again with the higher-ups who were questioning his every decision.

The car pulled out onto the road, and the sun reflected off the side. What looked like lettering glinted into view so quickly that if I'd blinked at the wrong time, I wouldn't have seen it. The only vehicles I knew with stealth lettering were unmarked police cars, but why would a police officer be tailing me? Erik might have sent someone to tag along after me and keep an eye on me before, but there was no way he could allocate police resources that way now with an internal investigation under way.

Wait a second...I thunked my head backward into my headrest, the memory of Elise scowling at me in the police station fresh in my mind. The police weren't tailing me. Elise Scott was. She must still think I'd had something to do with Noah's condition.

Normally I would have been cheesed, but right now I could use it to my advantage. I didn't relish heading off to talk to Noah's potential bookie on my own. If Elise wanted to know what I was up to, I'd offer to let her join me. Hopefully she'd see it as an olive branch and a sign of my innocence rather than as me trying too hard to win her over.

I threw on my four-ways and pulled off to the side of the road. I rolled down my window, and as the dark gray car drew even with mine, I stuck out my arm and flagged them down.

For two full breaths, the car didn't look like it was going to stop. It moved past me. Then the brake lights burst to life, and the car jerked to a stop. It backed up down the road until I was staring straight at the passenger's side window.

It rolled down.

The person inside was hard to see clearly in the shadows, but Elise's dark hair and tight bun seemed to be her trademark.

"How did you know?" she asked, her voice full of exasperation bordering on frustration.

I planted an elbow on the edge of my window. "I spotted the word *Police* in reflective paint."

"I meant how did you know I was following you."

"When you're raised by two criminal defense attorneys who want you to follow in their footsteps, you're drilled from the time you can talk to notice details, especially ones that seem out of the ordinary." I shrugged. "That, and I'm paranoid."

Elise huffed a sigh. "Would you tell me where you were headed if I asked?"

I gave her my best calling-a-truce smile. "I'll do better than that. I'll take you with me."

Elise decided I should ride with her rather than the other way around, which wasn't all that unexpected. Since she was convinced I'd whacked Noah in the head with something hard enough to crack his skull, she wasn't likely to let me drive her out to who knew where. If I was riding with her in a police cruiser, she maintained a certain level of control and safety.

We left my car in the furniture store parking lot, and I gave her the name and address of where I'd been headed.

"Hot date with a new boyfriend now that Noah's no use to you anymore?" Elise asked.

Her tone was ambiguous enough that, had I not known already how she felt about me, I wouldn't have known whether to interpret it as biting or teasing.

I chewed on the inside of my cheek—hard. Just because she chose to be snarky didn't mean I had to be. Had to remember that. "I'm actually hoping to find Noah's bookie."

The car swerved slightly and I grabbed the arm rest. Note to self: Don't drop surprising information on someone who's driving.

Before Elise could answer, her phone rang. She glanced at the screen and pulled the car off onto the shoulder. Whoever was calling, she didn't want to put it through the car. Were police cruisers even equipped with Bluetooth? Maybe I was reading too much into it.

"Hey, sweetie," Elise said to whoever was on the other end, her voice measurably softer than when she'd spoken to me.

She tilted her shoulders away from me. "No, don't worry. I promise the tooth fairy will still come even if you couldn't find your tooth."

Another pause as she must have been giving the child she was talking to a chance to reply.

"I'll be home before bedtime, okay?" she said. "Now go wash your face, and Grammie will help you with your spelling."

When she ended the call, she pulled back out onto the road, and at first, she refused to even look at me.

Finally she shot a hard look in my direction. "I don't spend a lot of time talking to my kids while I'm at work. But I'm a single mom, and I don't want them to worry I've taken off like their dad did."

She wouldn't get criticism from me, but I didn't know how to tell her so in a way that wouldn't sound patronizing.

"Why are you going to see Noah's bookie?" Elise asked, officially closing the window on any conversation about her kids. Any surprise she'd felt before was gone from her face and posture.

I tucked my hands under my thighs to warm them up. I'd forgotten my gloves in my car. "Erik...Interim Chief Higgins said there's nothing he could do to protect Noah from whoever might have hurt him until the situation is declared a crime. The only person I know of who'd want to hurt Noah is his bookie." That wasn't entirely true, but I wasn't going to tell Elise about the pictures of the girl-woman when Erik hadn't wanted to see them. "I figured that if I paid Noah's debt, he'd be safe."

"I see," Elise said in a way that reminded me eerily of Mark when he didn't know how to respond to whatever I'd just said.

Her lips thinned, and we rode the rest of the way to the Bar & Grill in an awkward silence. At least I found it awkward. I'd never enjoyed long silences to begin with, and certainly not with someone I barely knew. My instinct was to fill it with small talk, but Elise didn't strike me as a small-talk kind of woman.

She pulled the cruiser into a parking space to the side of the Bar & Grill.

She sat still instead of immediately releasing her seat belt and reaching for the door handle. "Do you want me to wait in the car?"

I paused with my own hand on the button for my seat belt. I'd assumed she'd insist on coming in and listening to everything I said in case I'd hired George Abbott to "deal with" Noah for some infraction.

Elise swept a hand down the front of her uniform. "He might not admit to being Noah's bookie if I'm with you."

Oohhh. I saw what she meant now. She must be working the odds in her head, and she'd decided that if it wasn't me who attacked Noah, the bookie was the next best option. She'd oblige me if it also helped her. "That might be for the best. I'll tell you if he says anything that could help the case."

I climbed from the car and went in the front door. Inside it smelled like French fries and beer, and the Bar & Grill was more crowded than I would have expected for a weekday afternoon. At least half the tables were filled, and ninety percent of the patrons were men.

Large-screen TVs lined all the walls, tuned in to different sporting events, from horse racing in what looked to be Florida to hockey. A couple of the stations even seemed to be playing foreign games, since I wasn't sure what game it was where men ran around with sticks that had little nets on the end.

There was no sign saying whether patrons should wait to be seated or not. I catalogued that fact away. While a few hungry travelers might straggle in, I had a feeling that this place tended to be frequented by regulars or those invited along by regulars.

If I was right, I'd have to break the privacy barrier, and it didn't bode well for being able to speak to George Abbott.

The bartender seemed to be around thirty-five or forty, close enough to my age that a little eyelash batting might help me out. Good thing I'd left Elise in the car. I certainly wouldn't rise any higher in her opinion of me if she saw what I was about to do.

I slid out of my jacket, glad I'd worn my fitted blue sweater, and fluffed my hair, saying a mental thank-you to my hairdresser Liz for being a miracle worker when it came to hair.

I drew my shoulders back into my best mother-trained posture and strode over to the bar. When the bartended looked in my direction, I flashed him a smile that I'm sure would have gotten me accused of flirting had Mark been with me.

His return smile wasn't exactly smarmy, but he wasn't looking me in the eyes either. Other parts of my anatomy clearly interested him more. "What can I get you?"

Asking for a water or a soda was sure to shut the conversation down before it even started—he'd probably think I was a police officer—but I didn't drink alcohol. My Uncle Stan's drinking had destroyed his heart, and that, along with his lecture, put the fear into me early enough in life that I'd decided to stay away from it. And, really, I was clumsy and goofy enough without alcohol adding to it.

But it left me with a quandary now. Maybe I could use it to curry some good will. "Is this the kind of place where I can buy the house a drink instead?"

His mouth quirked up on one side. "I never turn one down."

I slid a five dollar bill across the table and mentally crossed my fingers that would be enough. I had no idea what a drink would actually cost in a place like this.

He took it and poured himself a shot, then leaned a hip against the bar. "So you a narc? You're wasting your time if you are. Everything we sell here is licensed and legal."

And there went the subtle approach. Direct approach it was. I plopped my arms on the bar. "I'm not a cop. A friend of mine owes some money to George Abbott and I'm here to talk about clearing his debt."

His smirk clearly said that he thought "talk" was a euphemism for something else. I finally understood what people meant when they used the expression *I threw up a little bit in my mouth.*

"Follow me," he said.

I trailed behind him, suddenly glad I had Elise outside for backup if I needed her.

The bartended knocked on a door leading into a back room and a woman's voice answered. He stepped inside. He was back out too quickly for me to lose my nerve and go running to Elise.

He held open the door for me into a smallish office. The only person in the room was a petite red-head in her late thirties sitting behind the desk. Her nails had tiny daisies painted on them.

I glanced back at the bartender and he gave my chest one final stare before closing the door.

I turned back to the woman behind the desk. Something was definitely not right here. "I was hoping to meet with George Abbott."

The woman behind the desk rose to her feet. She was a good two inches shorter than I was and waif-thin. Even her button nose was tiny.

She held out a hand that I was almost afraid to shake for fear of snapping all her bird-like bones. "I'm Georgiana Abbott, and you are not who you claim to be. Anyone who actually owes me money knows that I'm a woman."

My mouth drooped open before I could catch it. My parents would have been so disappointed that I couldn't control my reaction better.

"So," *Georgiana* Abbott picked up a cup of what smelled like chamomile tea from her desk and took a sip, "who are you really and why are you here?"

That tickle in my throat that always preceded a stutter when I'd have to speak in front of a jury feathered its way up my throat.

*Pull it together, Nicole. This is no different from any other witness or suspect who wasn't what you expected them to be.*

My throat calmed down. I moved around her to the chair in front of her desk and sat without waiting for an invitation. "My name's Nicole Fitzhenry-Dawes"—I wagered that my hyphenated last name might actually help me this time— "and like I told your bartender, I'm here to pay the debt of a friend of mine."

Georgiana's eye roll clearly said *sure you are.* "I'm a very busy woman. Devin thinks you're a cop and that I should have you thrown out." She moved over to the window to the right of her desk and hooked a thumb toward it. Outside I could see part of a dark gray car. "But I think a cop wouldn't show up in an unmarked police car to do surveillance on me. So unless you're ready to tell me the real story, I'll have to ask you to leave."

She might have been the politest, most well-spoken bookie I'd ever met. Not that I'd met any bookies before this, but based on what I'd seen on TV. Which probably wasn't the most reliable resource.

Time to throw all my assumptions out the window and play it like I was as confident and cutthroat as she was.

I crossed my legs, folded my hands over my knee, and gave her my best imitation of my mom's don't-mess-with-me smile. "I'm a businesswoman as well, and earlier this week someone came onto my property and attacked one of my employees, a man by the name of Noah Miller. I think it was you, and so I'm here to settle Noah's debt with you so that we can make sure something like this doesn't happen again."

A muscle next to her eye twitched. "Someone hurt Noah?"

If it hadn't been for the twitch, I would have thought she was faking her shock. "You didn't know?"

She put a finger to her lips like she used to be a nail biter and the temptation was still hard to resist when she was under stress.

"Noah's one of my regulars." She sank down into her chair. "Was one of my regulars, I should say. He got mixed up with some girl and wanted to 'turn his life around.' I've heard that enough times from men who are right back here the next week, but Noah asked me to cut him off. He was so far in the hole by that point anyway that extending more credit to him would have been a stupid business decision, so I did what he asked. A couple of times he managed to sneak into a poker game in the back room, but other than that, he's been making regular payments ever since."

All her body language said she was telling the truth. Even her hand movements matched up the way they should with her words. I'd try one more thing to rattle her, but if she held solid to her story, I was inclined to think she'd had nothing to do with Noah's attack. "Why should I believe you that you didn't order the attack on Noah?"

Her confident smile peeked out again. "You know why. I'm a businesswoman. A man who can't work can't pay his debts, and that's bad business all around." She rolled her chair sideways and typed something into the laptop on her desk. "You're still welcome to pay his debt if you'd like, though. I never turn down a genuine offer of repayment."

I'd come here fully intending to pay off however much it took to keep Noah safe, but if Georgiana hadn't been behind the attack on Noah, I wasn't inclined to put Sugarwood at risk by draining my finances. If it was a small amount, though, I'd do it simply for the peace of mind. "How much does he owe?"

# Chapter 8

"So how much did Noah owe?" Elise asked as soon as I was back in the car.

My catatonic expression and zombie lumber must have given away that it was a lot more than I'd been expecting. "More than he earns in two years."

For a second, her expression said she thought I was messing with her. "Wait. You're serious?"

I filled Elise in on everything that had gone on while I was inside, minus the part where I tried to flirt my way in to see "George" Abbott.

"Are you still going to pay it?"

I shrugged. Uncle Stan had left me his life insurance policy and retirement investments, but they hadn't been a huge amount of cash. Most of what he'd set aside during his years as a cardiologist he spent buying Sugarwood. If I drained what I had to pay Noah's debt, and we had a bad year, I'd have nothing in reserve to make sure Sugarwood stayed afloat.

Elise was still waiting for an answer from me, one eyebrow cocked.

"Because it's so much, I can't make that decision without talking to Russ since it'd drain the cushion I'd planned to keep to protect Sugarwood. I don't think Georgiana Abbott did it, but I'm not naturally a risk-taker either. Paying her would make sure Noah was safe from her at least."

"You must really love him."

I choked on my own spit and coughed for a full thirty seconds. Red alert sirens went off in my brain like it was the bridge of the USS *Enterprise*. That statement felt suspiciously like she was trying to trick me into admitting a relationship with Noah. But I had no relationship with Noah, and asking the same question a thousand different ways wasn't going to change that.

How could she still think I'd had something to do with this? Surely after I'd gone to all this trouble to meet with Noah's bookie, she should realize I hadn't been the one to attack him.

"I'm not in love with Noah." I kept my voice even, since I was sure any sign of emotion at all would be willfully misinterpreted. "He's my employee, and he needed help."

Elise rolled her eyes in a way that clearly said she thought I was a terrible liar. Which was ironic, really. I was a decent liar when I needed to be, and this time I was telling the truth. But nothing I did seemed to change this woman's opinion.

I shoved my hands into the pockets of my jacket. Was this still about me being a Fair Haven newcomer and therefore inherently untrustworthy? A lot of the people in town had been generous and open, but an equal number had treated me with suspicion and sometimes outright contempt because I wasn't one of them. I'd been told that was normal for a tourist town. With the number of strangers who passed through in a year, the permanent residents learned to trust only each other.

Up until now, I'd been patient, but I'd had about all of it that I was going to take.

I shifted toward her as much as the seatbelt would allow. "Look, I know I haven't lived in Fair Haven for hundreds of years like everyone else, but it's my home now, too. If you have any real reason to believe I had something to do with this or to just not like me, fine. Otherwise, stop treating me like everything I say has about as much truth to it as a celebrity gossip magazine."

"I have plenty of reasons not to like you."

Her voice was filled with enough venom that it could have kept medical researchers working for years.

I shrank back. That was not the reaction I'd been expecting. "You don't even know me."

"I know all I need to know about you."

Heat crept up my neck and into my face. Elise had said something about my reputation the first time we'd met. I hadn't paid much attention to it then. Now all the old insecurities that I was supposed to have left back in Virginia threatened to choke me.

Fair Haven, for all its flaws, was my fresh start. If I already had a reputation—one that would make Elise dislike me this much—then what chance did I have? Small towns had long memories. If you stole a jar of jam as a kid, you'd be known as a thief until the day you died.

So basically, I'd moved to a place that was like being perpetually stuck in elementary school.

Screw that. I hadn't enjoyed elementary school the first time around.

"All you have is gossip. If you have so many reasons not to like me, you should at least make sure they're true."

Elise's hands tensed around the steering wheel. "Fine. You're a criminal defense attorney, working hard to put scumbags back on the street, undoing all the hard work law enforcement put into catching them."

Aside from the fact that she'd used the word *scumbags* like we were on an 80s cop show, I could see why this would bother her. My dad always used the argument that everyone deserved fair representation, but part of why I'd left my old life was because I didn't agree. I couldn't continue defending clients I knew were guilty.

"I'm not a lawyer anymore."

Elise gave me a sidelong glance. "Uh huh. You defended a client last month."

I had done that, but not in the way she'd taken it. Tension built in the space between my eyes, and I rubbed at it with my fingers. The truth could be so easily twisted. How could I ever hope to unravel it?

But since Elise seemed to be the only one as interested as I was in investigating what had really happened to Noah—and the only one giving me a chance to explain myself—I'd give it a try.

"That case never went to trial. I didn't hide my client's guilt." It'd been a special situation, but I didn't know how to explain that to Elise. I'd only done it because that was how I could bring justice to a good man who'd died and also try to make it as easy as possible on a woman who'd made a single bad decision in a moment of anger. I didn't know if Elise's worldview allowed for enough grayscale to understand that, but she should understand that I'd never tried to pretend my client was innocent. "Despite how much I liked her, my legal counsel was to turn herself in, confess, and accept the punishment for her crime."

Elise licked her lips and shifted in her seat. She kept her gaze on the road. "Okay, then why do you keep going out with Erik—Chief Higgins—when you're clearly not interested in commitment? Maybe in the big city it's okay to date multiple men and then drop them when you lose interest, but we're a small town. You hurt more than just the men you're leading on."

I pressed my fingers into the side of my nose and held them there.

She'd had to correct herself to call Erik *Chief Higgins*. That sort of slip usually happened when people thought about someone one way privately and had to address them a different way publicly. I hadn't seen them together, so I couldn't be too hard on myself for not figuring it out, but Elise's problems with me had nothing to do with me being a lawyer or even a newcomer to town. We'd hit the real reason she disliked me so much.

She was interested in Erik, and she thought I was stringing him along. She'd probably been hoping I was in love with Noah and would leave Erik alone.

I was in love with someone else, but it wasn't Noah.

I leaned my temple against the window and let the coolness seep into my hot skin. This was such a mess. It was no wonder I'd had so much trouble making friends since coming here. The locals thought I was a heartbreaker, as my grandmother—and probably Elise—would have said.

Part of me wanted to plug my ears and hum rather than hear what else was being said about me, but I couldn't sort this out until I knew the full extent of it. "Multiple men?"

Her gaze slid toward me and little creases formed between her eyebrows. "Chief Higgins. Noah. The guy who runs your rental shop. Mark Cavanaugh."

"Oh good Lord." I buried my face in my hands to give myself a moment of privacy. Every innocent thing I did had probably been warped beyond recognition. "People are saying I'm fooling around with Dave? He's nearly ten years younger than I am."

"Cougars are a thing now." Elise's voice carried a shrug.

I sucked in a fortifying breath and put my hands back in my lap. At least I knew the worst of it now. "Thank you for telling me."

"So how much of it is true?"

Her voice had softened, like my obvious distress had earned me a little compassion at least. And had convinced her that some of the gossip might be off-base.

Her lips twitched. "You did say I should ask."

I might soon regret that. "Very little. I never went out with Dave or Noah. They're my employees, and my parents taught me to keep those lines firm."

The tightness in her arms and upper body telegraphed that I hadn't addressed the person she most interested in.

"Erik and I went out a couple of times when I was first in Fair Haven, but then we mutually decided that we were better as friends. As you might have guessed, I don't have a lot of those in Fair Haven yet, so I spend quite a bit of time with the ones I do have."

I'd swear her control slipped enough that she almost smiled. Next time Erik and I had breakfast, I was going to do some gentle nudging to suggest he might want to ask her out sometime. I could see them as a couple. They were both hard-shelled with a soft interior.

The furniture store where we'd left my car came into view ahead of us, and Elise pulled up alongside my car.

Then she turned off the ignition.

My stomach tightened. There was only one reason for her to not simply put the car into park while I got out. Our conversation about my reputation wasn't over.

"You left one out," Elise said, the edge back to her voice.

I'd left out Mark intentionally. Elise might not be the best detective on the planet, but my feelings for Mark apparently broadcast themselves like a lighthouse beacon whenever I was around him or talked about him. Erik noticed it. Russ noticed it. I had the uncomfortable suspicion that even Oliver had noticed it.

Why would she care that I hadn't explained Mark? Her interest in Erik precluded any interest in Mark, so it couldn't be that. It could be that he was a married man, and I shouldn't be corrupting one of the most well-liked men in town.

I had no answer to give that wouldn't destroy the speck of goodwill I'd earned from her in easing her mind about Erik. "I left one out."

I rested my hand on the door handle. Maybe I should get out and let her draw whatever conclusions she wanted.

Elise's police-issued shoes squeaked on the floorboard. "You haven't been in town long enough to know this, but my maiden name was Cavanaugh."

Ugg. I should have recognized it sooner. The dark hair. The way they both had super-human control over their eyebrows. And the slight geeky awkwardness in the things they said.

But I knew Mark didn't have sisters. "Mark's your cousin."

"Mark, Grant, and I were born the same year, so we grew up more like siblings."

The implication in her words was *we look out for each other.*

A lump grew in my throat. It must be nice to have family who had your back. Someone like Elise couldn't possibly know how lonely it was to have very little family and now very few friends as well. When I announced I was giving up law and moving to Michigan to run a maple syrup farm, I'd quickly found out that most of the people I thought were my friends in DC weren't my friends at all. And I hadn't spoken more than a smattering of words to my dad in nearly six months. That made for a particularly fun Thanksgiving and Christmas.

I was done talking about this. I didn't owe her an explanation of my feelings for Mark, cousin or not. Where Mark was concerned, she could draw whatever conclusions she wanted. Most of them would probably be true anyway.

Elise started the car before I could tighten my hand on the door handle to open the door. "I believe you now. That there's nothing going on between you and Noah or you and Erik or you and Dave from the rental shop."

She'd left one out. And I'd no doubt she'd done it intentionally.

I climbed out of the car and walked around the back. As I came even with the driver's side of her car, she rolled down the window.

"Hey, Nicole?"

I stopped. Hopefully she wasn't about to lecture me because I didn't want to embarrass myself more by crying in front of her. It should be enough that I'd left Mark alone, for the most part. How I still felt shouldn't matter to her as long as I did the right thing and stayed far away from him.

Elise smiled at me. A tiny Cavanaugh dimple formed in her cheek. I blinked rapidly to make sure it wasn't my imagination. If she'd ever smiled at me before this moment, I would have seen the resemblance between her and Mark right away.

"I think," she said, "that in an alternate reality, you and I might have been friends."

# Chapter 9

I climbed into my car, dropped my purse on top of the evidence folders on the passenger's seat, and stopped, my keys halfway to the ignition, dangling in mid-air.

*He got mixed up with some girl*, Georgiana Abbott had said.

*Mixed up* could mean a lot of things, and the girl Georgiana mentioned might not be the same one as the girl-woman in the picture. It did mean that whoever hurt Noah might be someone from his past that he'd been in trouble with.

I couldn't show the evidence I'd collected to Elise any more than I could show it to Erik. I still needed to put it back like he asked me to. But Elise had proven that she actively wanted to solve this case and was treating it as attempted murder rather than as an accident. She might be willing to check into Noah's past and see if he had any kind of a criminal record.

Elise's headlights were already at my rear bumper. I didn't have her cell phone number, and I wasn't about to risk anyone's career by trying to reach her at the police station. It was now or wait until I could arrange an accidental meeting. Every hour we waited was another hour Noah's life was in danger.

I dove from my car and sprinted toward the back end, waving my arms, as Elise's car pulled out of the parking space and turned in my direction.

The cruiser screeched to a halt, skidding forward. I jumped back.

The driver's side door heaved open and Elise bolted out, her angry cop mask firmly back in place. "I thought you said you weren't a risk-taker. What do you think you're doing? I could have run you down and then we'd both be fodder for the rumor mill."

I clamped a hand over my mouth, but a snicker broke lose anyway. That was too funny an idea to hold inside. I could see the headlines now: *Cop Runs Down Police Chief's Alleged Girlfriend in Jealous Rage.*

Elise planted her hands on her hips. Her headlights blinded me enough that I could only see her silhouette and not her expression.

I stepped around the lights and joined her next to her open door. It might have been my father's DNA in me, but I didn't like to be at a disadvantage to anyone. Not being able to see her face put me at a distinct disadvantage.

With the headlights no longer giving me camera-flash syndrome, I could see her pursed lips.

"Is it safe to say that you no longer consider me a suspect in Noah's attack?" I asked.

Elise sighed, but the note underneath it was good-humored this time. "I suppose so."

"I think you might want to do a background check on Noah to see if he has any sort of a criminal record." I'd save the detail about the girl-woman for now. Mentioning it would only put Elise in a bad position because then she'd want to see the pictures. "Georgiana Abbott said something about him being in trouble with a woman, and that's what made him get help for his gambling problem. It could also point to someone who might have wanted him dead."

Some of that was extrapolation, but my heart was in the right place, so that had to count for something. Besides, Elise would have wanted to know why I thought a police check on Noah might yield pertinent information. By feeding her that up-front, I kept control of the conversation, and hopefully she wouldn't ask any follow-up questions that I'd have a hard time answering without telling her about the pictures I found.

Elise gave a sharp nod. "Thanks. I appreciate the help. I'm not..." She looked over her shoulder like another police officer might have snuck up on us while we

weren't watching. "I'm not actually supposed to be investigating, but Mark is sure this wasn't an accident,
and Russ is more worried for Noah than he wants to
admit."

Olive branch offered and accepted. It felt nice to
not be at odds with *someone* in this town at least. "All
I've wanted from the start was to help."

"I see that now." Elise reached into her pockets and
pulled out a card. She handed it to me. "My cell phone
number in case you think of anything else. I'll give you
a call if I find out anything."

I was helping bottle maple syrup the next afternoon
when my cell phone rang. I didn't recognize the number, so I let it go to voicemail. I'd slacked off on my role
at Sugarwood enough that I didn't feel right taking
calls when I should be working.

The third time the number vibrated my phone, I
held it up at Russ with a hands-in-the-air shrug and
ducked into the storage room.

"Nicole Fitzhenry-Dawes."

"It's Elise."

Her voice was so low I could barely hear her, and
there was noise in the background of wherever she was,
people talking. One of the background voices sounded
a bit like Quincey Dornbush, so my best guess was that
she was at the police station.

And there was only one reason I could think of that she'd be calling me so soon and wouldn't want to be overheard. "Did you find something?"

"Yeah. Noah doesn't have a record per se, but he was charged with statutory rape. The name of the girl isn't in the file since she was a minor, and apparently the charges were dropped because the girl insisted Noah hadn't touched her. It was her father who went to the police, claiming Noah had harmed his daughter."

My stomach turned queasy and I sank down with my back against one of the black metal shelves. "Does it say how old the girl was?"

"Fifteen."

If Russ knew about this and hadn't told me, we were going to have words. And I still couldn't show Elise the pictures I'd found. The girl-woman in them had looked older than fifteen to me, but I had noticed that teenagers in general were looking a lot older a lot faster than they had when I was a kid. If it wasn't the same girl, we were looking at something worse—a pattern. "How long ago was this?"

"Three years."

"That seems like a long time to wait to seek revenge after Noah was cleared."

"I was thinking the same thing. But if we assume that he was guilty and the girl didn't want to admit to it, then it could have been the family of another underage girl who came after him this time."

That meant tracking down every teenage girl Noah had any sustained contact with.

A burning sensation shot up my throat and I swallowed hard. "We regularly hire teenagers for part-time jobs here. I'll get you a list. I imagine you'll want to talk to them."

"This should be enough to convince Er—Chief Higgins to open a criminal case. It'd help if we could talk to the girl involved with the initial charge. At the very least, we could figure out more about Noah's type and patterns for how he might start a relationship."

"We could ask Oliver Miller, Noah's cousin, if he knows who the girl was."

I thought Elise might have groaned, but I wasn't sure. "I know who Oliver is. Are you willing to try talking to him? He won't talk to me. After he got fired, he turned everyone who still works here into a villain. Except Mark. No one hates Mark."

It was almost like she enjoyed throwing Mark's name around to see if she could get a reaction from me. I wasn't about to react.

Russ stuck his head in the storeroom door and tapped his watch. I held up one finger, and he closed the door again.

His constant warnings about ruining the reputations of innocent people suddenly played in my head. "I'll talk to Oliver, but do you think we can keep this quiet? The girl did say Noah hadn't touched her. Maybe he was innocent."

"Maybe." Elise huffed out a breath. "I don't know what to hope for here. My kids love Noah. If he was innocent of the charges, we're back to the beginning on who might have wanted to hurt him."

According to Russ, he *and* Uncle Stan knew about the charges brought against Noah, but they believed him when he said nothing had happened between him and the girl.

"We wouldn't have hired him otherwise," Russ said, his hands out like he was pleading with me to believe him. "And we watched Noah close afterward anyway. Nothing he's done said those accusations might be true."

I rubbed my hands over my face. That might have been enough for me once. But even though I didn't want our investigation to hurt Noah's reputation, I also had more people to think about now. Employees who depended on me for their livelihood.

I used to hear my parents talk about it sometimes, how every decision they made about their business could impact their employees, but I hadn't understood it until my decisions might mean someone couldn't pay their electricity bill anymore. "You took a huge risk. Do you know what's going to happen to this business if it turns out Noah acted inappropriately toward a minor?"

The look on his face—like he'd taken a punch to his man parts—told me he did. We were a maple syrup farm, but at least a quarter of our revenue came from family events like the tours. No one would bring their children to a place that had knowingly harbored a sex offender. And no one would let their daughters work here anymore, either.

This was the worst possible year for it to happen, too. Russ had been on the phone with the manufacturer of our sap lines half the afternoon yesterday. The lines kept bursting, costing us time, money, and production. They were sending someone out to examine the lines later this week to see if we'd ended up with a faulty production batch.

"We understood the risks," Russ said, "but your uncle and I also thought it was the right thing to do to give a person a chance to prove themselves and to let them know someone believed them."

A chance to prove themselves. It was what I'd demanded from Elise yesterday when she'd wanted to believe the rumors about me without seeking out the truth.

Great. Now I felt like a hypocrite.

Of course, I'd only be a hypocrite if Noah were innocent the way I was of the accusations Elise made. "Do you know who the girl in question was?"

Russ wagged his head. "Noah wouldn't tell us. Said he knew how easily things could get out, and he didn't want to do that to her reputation."

I'd have to talk to Oliver and hope his tolerance of me held out. This time, though, I needed to speak to him in person so I could show him the picture of the girl and see if he recognized her.

# Chapter 10

We'd faxed a list of former and current female teenage employees over to Elise, but it was two days before I could get away from Sugarwood, and even then, I only had one hour. The pace at Sugarwood had been laid-back my first month here, and I hadn't realized how that would change when syrup season actually hit.

I climbed into my car, still dressed in my working clothes, smelling of maple syrup. With the time I had, I could only go one place—the hospital or Quantum Mechanics. I'd called the hospital on my walk from the sugar shack to the car, and so I knew Oliver wasn't there. If I went to visit Noah, I'd lose my chance to ask Oliver about the girl in the photo and whether he knew the name of the girl who'd been involved in Noah's statutory rape charge.

As much as it felt like I should visit Noah, he wouldn't know I was there. The more logical use of my time seemed to be to try to track down who had hurt him.

I reached the point where I'd have to turn away from the hospital if I was heading for Quantum Mechanics. I threw on my signal and made the turn.

Seeing how bare Noah's house was, he'd probably have wanted me to take the practical option if he'd been able to cast a vote.

I pulled my car into a space at Quantum Mechanics and climbed out. This was the first time I'd been here without my car in a shambles.

I didn't recognize the man at the desk inside. My suspicion was that they didn't have an actual receptionist or secretary. From the times I'd been here, it seemed like the mechanics each took a turn manning the desk. Erik had said something the second time my car was in the shop about Tony liking his mechanics to have contact with the customers. His theory was that it made them aware that there were lives at stake if they didn't do their job well.

I asked if I could talk to Oliver for a minute, and the desk mechanic went into the shop. It was only after he was already gone that I wanted to kick myself for what this might look like. With the rumors that were already flying around town about me, asking for Oliver at work might add his name to the list. I should have at least told the desk mechanic that I was Noah's boss and I needed to check something with Oliver about Noah.

Someone needed to invent future 20/20 glasses to prevent situations like this.

Oliver came out from the shop, wiping his hands methodically on a rag as though he hated the touch of grease on his skin. Even though getting fired from his job at the police station had been his own fault, I could understand how he might feel resentful if he'd had to return to a job he didn't enjoy. Of course, I was speculating. Maybe Oliver loved fixing cars and only changed jobs for some other reason...but based on the way he was scowling at his dirty hands, I doubted it.

"Has something happened to Noah?" Oliver asked.

I cringed internally. I was 0 for 2 today in considering how other people might interpret my actions. "I'm sure the hospital would call you rather than me."

He slow-blinked at me like I might be stupid. Either that or he was baffled by what other reason could possibly be good enough for me to interrupt him at work. If he'd heard the rumors about me, he might even think I was here because I was romantically interested in him. At this point, nothing people in this town assumed about me would surprise me.

I slid the picture of Noah and the girl-woman from my purse. "I did have a couple of questions for you about Noah, though. We're getting close to being able to open an official case so the police can search for who hurt him."

Another round of slow blinks like that wasn't news to him. Since he'd worked at the police station, he probably was smart enough to allow the police to do their work, and trusted that they'd take care of everything. He might have more common sense than I did. I kept butting in.

Should I tell him that the police asked me to come or would that make him less likely to tell me anything, the way Elise feared? This was already going to be an awkward enough conversation without me making it worse by a poor judgment call. I'd skip mentioning the police for now, since Elise wasn't even technically supposed to be investigating herself.

"In looking at who might have wanted to hurt Noah," I licked my lips to buy myself some time to find the right words, "some things in his past other than his gambling addiction came up. There were some accusations brought against him."

The corners of Oliver's lips turned down and his upper eyelids drooped, bringing his eyes to the size of most people rather than his usual shocked expression. "Yeah, that."

He must have been taking lessons from Russ because that was as close to a non-answer as one could get. I held up the picture for him to see.

"Do you know the name of the girl who was involved in the charges?" I tapped a finger next to the face of the girl-woman in the photo. "Or do you know who this woman is?"

Oliver's lip muscles twitched in a mini-expression of emotion. My dad had always said mini-expressions were essential to watch for when examining a witness on the stand because they'd point out the areas you needed to follow up on. They were leakage of an emotion a person wanted to hide or repress.

I had no idea what emotion Oliver wanted to suppress—it could be as simple as not wanting to seem disgusted at a cousin he cared about—but he definitely knew something about the situation, the girl in the photo, or both.

The door that led back to the shop swung open and Tony shuffled out.

He raised a hand and gave me his tiny, shy smile. "Hey, Nicole. No more car accidents, I hope. You here to pick up Mark's truck for him? That part's been delayed again, so it's not ready yet."

His gaze shifted to the photo in my hand, and the tone underneath his skin went from peachy-pink to washed-out grey.

The back of my throat burned and saliva flooded my mouth as though I might be sick. Whether or not Oliver knew the girl-woman in the photo, Tony definitely did.

"Are you here about a problem with your car?" There was a brittleness to Tony's voice that was unnatural. I'd never heard him anything other than soft-spoken. "Otherwise, we're busy today and I need all my employees working."

I stuffed the photo back in my purse, not worrying about whether I bent it or not and suddenly grateful that I'd chosen one of the more innocent pictures. For a second I considered fibbing and saying that Oliver was helping me book an oil change for my car. Given that Tony had seen me showing Oliver the photo, though, that would only draw even more attention to it.

"I'm sorry." I swung my purse over my shoulder. "That was thoughtless of me. I'll let you both get back to work."

I hurried to my car, got in, and sucked in a huge breath. My lungs felt like I'd forgotten to breathe for a full minute. Tony's reaction wasn't good. At all. He'd been upset by the picture of Noah and the girl-woman, and that suggested she meant something to him. A daughter, maybe, or a niece. She'd be the right age for either.

And whoever the girl-woman was, Tony wasn't over whatever happened between her and Noah. If she was the same girl whose father had brought statutory rape charges against Noah, then I knew, based on the photos, that both Noah and the girl had lied.

The question was, would Tony or someone else close to him have acted to punish Noah after all these years?

# Chapter 11

My brain wanted to panic and jump to all sorts of conclusions. Like that Tony had finally snapped and attacked Noah. Like that I was once again going to have to decide between hiding the truth and letting a good but guilty person walk free.

In this case, if Noah had been inappropriate with a girl Tony cared about, I couldn't even blame him. Had it been my daughter, and the legal system wasn't able to take action against him, I might have taken matters into my own hands, too, rather than allow him to walk free and do the same thing to other girls.

Then again, in this town, the quickest path to destroying anyone seemed to be through the rumor mill. Tony could have—no, he couldn't. He couldn't say anything about what Noah had done publicly without also bringing the kind of attention he probably didn't want onto the girl.

I told my brain to knock it off and started my car. I didn't even know for sure that the girl was related to Tony. Figuring out her name was the first thing I needed to do. Once I identified her, I'd hand this over to Elise.

Maybe it was the coward's way out, but then it'd be her call, not mine, as to what to do about it next.

I turned onto the street, but drove well below the speed limit. I should return to Sugarwood, but if I did, it could be days before I could follow up on this lead. And now Tony knew I was looking. If he'd had something to do with Noah's attack, who knew what that might drive him to do.

Something Oliver said earlier came back to me. Noah had supposedly been fired from Quantum Mechanics for stealing, but what could he have stolen, really? I doubted there was a black market around here for wrenches and steering shafts. As far as I saw, they only accepted payment by credit card, so Noah couldn't have been skimming cash.

What if the "fired for stealing" story was a cover? Noah might have been fired because of the situation with the girl in the photo.

If I had the time, I could go to the Fair Haven library and look through the high school yearbooks and church photo directories.

My phone vibrated in my pocket. I put on my four-ways and parked at the edge of the road.

*Inspector here to look at the sap lines,* the text from Russ said. *Need you back at Sugarwood ASAP.*

Figuring out who the girl in the photo was would have to wait.

"How can there be nothing structurally wrong with our lines?" I asked as Russ and I stood out front of the sugar shack, watching the inspector from the sap line manufacturer pull away. "Are you sure he's not just saying that so they don't have to take on the cost of replacing all our lines?"

Russ' hair already stuck out in three directions, but he ran his fingers through it again. With all that had been going wrong at the farm so far, I had a suspicion he hadn't showered in a few days. "I watched him run all the tests, and he showed me samples he brought from the factory. There's no difference."

If I hadn't figured out a couple of hours ago that Tony had something to do with the girl in Noah's photo, I might have wondered if my day could get any worse. In retrospect, the blow of the mysteriously faulty sap lines lessened slightly in comparison. "So what do we do?"

"He suggested trapping and relocating squirrels who might be gnawing on the lines."

Oh dear Lord. Now I'd heard it all. "He wants us to set up little live traps in our *bush* to catch squirrels. There have to be hundreds of squirrels out there. It's a bush, not a city garden."

I didn't even try to squelch the hysterical note to my voice. I needed to release some of my pent-up worry and frustration, and it might as well be over the fact that our best hope for salvaging our sugar season basically told us we had a squirrel infestation.

It almost made me wish I was a drinker...which actually was probably why Uncle Stan had put the fear of God into me when I was a teenager about drinking at all. Given that I was already a chronic overeater when stressed, I'd have been an alcoholic by now if he hadn't.

"Trapping and releasing the squirrels isn't practical," Russ said, as if he thought I might be seriously considering it. "I'm not even sure I'm convinced that's the cause. I've worked here my whole adult life. I don't see why we'd have more squirrels this year than any other, or why they'd take an extra-special interest in our sap lines."

So we didn't know what was damaging our lines, which meant we also didn't know how to stop it, and we'd continue hemorrhaging sap until we did. I had to ask the obvious question. "What does this mean for our production this year?"

"You don't want to know."

"Russ." I infused my voice with the warning tone I'd heard my mother use whenever I'd stepped across her quilt-pattern of lines.

Russ bobbed his head. "Right. Partner."

We were making progress there, at least.

"We'll have to run the numbers." His finger moved through the air as though he were already running sums in his head. "We have a cushion that can see us through one bad year, but it's going to be tight if we also continue to lose tours with Noah gone."

Russ and I had talked about me paying off Noah's debt to Georgiana Abbott, and with the shakiness of the current season, he'd advised me against it. Not only did he think, based on what I'd told him, that Georgiana hadn't hurt Noah, but he didn't want to see me in financial trouble if Noah passed on.

I'd felt like an awful human being for following his advice, but now it seemed he'd been right. We might need my savings to keep Sugarwood running.

In the meantime, we needed to do some damage control. "I can start leading the tours myself. I know quite a bit about syrup production now, and Noah taught me how to tack up the horses and drive the sleigh."

"You're the best choice for it," Russ said.

I decided not to ask whether it was because I was the best with the horses or I was the least experienced with the hands-on production and therefore was the one who could best be spared. "I'll talk to Tom

McClanahan as well. Uncle Stan left me some money that I should have access to assuming the estate is fully settled now."

The first opening Tom McClanahan had in his schedule was three days later.

I showed up at his office five minutes before my scheduled appointment time.

Ashley glanced up from her computer screen, her face looking like she'd recently had another Botox treatment. As usual, her clothes were borderline not suitable for work with the amount of cleavage they showed.

"Can I help you?" she asked in a tone that implied my very existence was wasting her time.

In a way, it was a shame I didn't have Mark with me. Ashley at least attempted to be pleasant when he was around.

"I have a three o'clock appointment with Tom."

"Mmmm." Ashley tapped her keyboard and the gold bangles on her wrist clinked together. "No, you don't, and he's fully booked today. You'll have to actually make an appointment and come back then."

Ashley had been the one who answered the phone when I called and who booked my appointment. She knew full well that I'd booked an appointment today. The fact that I wasn't actually on the schedule had to be intentional.

*If you react, she wins*, my mother's voice said in my head.

The bell above the door jingled, probably signaling the arrival of the people Ashley had given my appointment slot to. Tom always came out of his office to greet his appointments himself and usher them in. I could circumvent Ashley's nasty trick despite her best efforts.

I blasted Ashley with my best smile, one that I hoped would make it seem like I thought this was an honest mistake. "That's okay that you misplaced it. I'm sure once I tell Tom what happened, he'll squeeze me in. I'll just grab him for a second when he comes out."

It was hard to tell because of her fake spray tan, but I thought she might have paled a shade. She snatched up the phone on her desk. "I'll call him and see what he can do."

It turned out I was showing my ignorance of estate law by even going. I wouldn't have been able to add Russ as a part-owner of Sugarwood had the estate not already been settled.

I came out of his office less than five minutes after I went in. I'd told Russ it would be an hour before I was back. The responsible part of me said I should head back to Sugarwood early regardless. The paranoid part of me said I needed to see if I could find out the identity of the girl-woman in Noah's photo.

The Fair Haven library was one street over from Tom McClanahan's office. One of the things I loved about small town living was how close everything was. Back in DC, I'd often have to be in the car for forty-five minutes to reach something that wasn't any farther away than one side of Fair Haven to the other.

Had it not been winter, I would have walked. As it was, I drove the short distance. My lips and hands were already chapped beyond repair.

The Fair Haven library smelled like old paper and lemon Pinesol. The best part of law school, in my opinion, was access to the library. The smell and the quiet were soothing.

Fair Haven's library had the smell, but not the quiet. A cluster of children giggled and ducked through the children's section to the right of the front door. Based on the fact that only one harried-looking adult supervised them, they might have been an after-school program. At least they were at the library. There were worse places a kid could be after school let out.

The librarian at the check-out desk pointed me toward the archives—second floor, toward the back. Unfortunately, none of the records had been archived online, which meant I'd be searching through records by hand rather than being able to search for Tony's last name.

The second floor had the peace I'd been hoping for. I easily found the shelves where they stored the Fair Haven yearbooks dating back to the first one they'd ever printed.

The only certain date I had was that three years ago the girl Noah was accused of being improper with had been fifteen. That likely made her a sophomore. I took the yearbook for that year off the shelf and wiggled the now-wrinkled photo from my purse.

I'd know quickly whether my suspicions were right or not.

I flipped to the sophomore class and to the R's, wagering the girl would have the same last name as Tony. A younger version of the face in Noah's photo stared back at me.

I pulled out my phone, entered Elise's number, and texted *The girl was Stacey Rathmell.* Elise would know who I meant.

And now I'd pray that I'd been wrong about what Tony might have been willing to do to avenge her and stop the man he believed had hurt her.

I called Russ' cell phone on my way back to Sugarwood. With the number of times he'd mentioned my visit with Tom McClanahan the past couple of days, I knew he was worrying about the implications if we didn't have a slightly larger slush fund should Sugarwood have a few unprofitable years. I didn't want to leave him wondering any longer, especially since I'd have to swing by my house to change clothes and let the dogs out before I returned to work.

He sounded out of breath when he answered. My phone was Bluetooth-enabled, so his voice played through my speakers, magnifying every huffing intake of air.

"Are you okay?" I asked and pushed my car a little faster. I wouldn't get a ticket at this speed in DC, but in Fair Haven...well, I'd have to hope no one spotted me.

"The reverse osmosis machine's making a funny hissing whistle. Normally Noah'd handle it, but with him not here, I'm trying to figure out what might be wrong with it. I was all the way under the machine before you called. Had to crawl back out to answer."

This had to be some bad cosmic joke. Shouldn't the fact that I'd started going to church mean that my life got better? If Mark had still been my friend, I would have asked him—he'd had a good answer for all my other questions about God—but asking Mark wasn't an option anymore. I could ask the pastor, but I wasn't sure if there was some protocol to that or not.

"I'll let you get back to it," I said to Russ. "I just called to tell you—"

A boom ricocheted through my car speakers.

# Chapter 12

I screamed and jerked my steering wheel. My car skidded onto the icy shoulder. I slammed on my brakes, but they locked and I kept sliding, right into the snowbank in the ditch. The call with Russ had dropped.

I sat there, my pulse pounding loud enough in my ears that it sounded like an avalanche bearing down on me. And all I could think was that my air bag hadn't deployed again, and it probably should have, because I was in a ditch. And I could be dead right now. And Russ might be dead.

Something had exploded at Sugarwood.

My hands were shaking so badly that it took me two tries to correctly dial 9-1-1. I explained to the dis-

patcher what I'd heard. He assured me they'd send police, an ambulance, and a fire truck.

I hung up without telling him that I was in a ditch.
I could call back if it came to that, but if I did, I'd have
to wait for police and maybe even an ambulance for
myself. I was pretty sure I hadn't hit my head on the
steering wheel, so I should be fine.

What I needed was to get home and find out what
had happened.

The person I most wanted to call was Mark, but I
couldn't, not even now. I tried to call Erik, but as was
the new normal since he'd become interim chief, his
line was busy. I went straight to voicemail. I didn't
bother leaving a message.

Instead, I called the only other person I had to call
anymore. At least the only person who might be able to
get to me fast enough and get me to Sugarwood to find
out what had happened.

"Scott," Elise's voice said.

Considering how much she'd disliked me less than
two weeks ago, she was remarkably patient as I blurted
out my story again, this time adding in the fact that I'd
driven my car into a ditch. In the back of my mind, I
recognized the tone in her voice as the same one she'd
used on the child who'd called her about the missing
tooth. The random thought that she was probably a
great mom flitted through my mind.

Elise told me I should get out of my car to wait for
her. She didn't want me inside with the engine running

in case the exhaust pipe was plugged by snow and I asphyxiated myself. It was rare to meet someone with nearly as paranoid a mind as I had.

She was right. Had circumstances been different, we might have been friends.

The shoulder I'd dislocated last fall ached as I undid my seatbelt and climbed up out of the ditch. Fortunately for me, temperatures had to come up above freezing for the sap to run, which meant I wasn't in sub-zero temperatures while waiting.

I tried calling Russ' cell phone back twice in the time it took Elise to reach me. No answer. With each failed attempt, my heart climbed higher in my throat until I could barely swallow around it.

When Elise rolled up, her lights were on and she stopped the car only long enough for me to jump in and buckle up.

"Have you heard anything yet?" I asked.

She shook her head. The contrast between her dark hair and her pale skin was starker than when I'd last seen her. It took me a minute to remember that Russ had once been engaged to Mark's aunt before she died from cancer. It could have been a maternal aunt, but it might have also been a shared aunt, so Elise might view Russ with the same affection that Mark did, as a person who would have been family had life gone differently.

She was probably more scared right now than I was, and I had no comfort to give her.

As we pulled into the parking lot out front of the sugar shack, we couldn't get anywhere near the building. A firetruck and Fair Haven police cruiser blocked the way, and an ambulance was parked to one side beyond them. I caught a glimpse of Officer Quincey Dornbush's balding head bobbing around in the crowd of milling people.

Thankfully, no flames licked from the building. Whatever had exploded either hadn't caused a larger fire or the fire department had already put it out.

We jogged toward the chaos, Elise leading the way and parting the crowd in a way that I wouldn't have been able to. The flashing lights and impending sunset gave the whole setting the feel of a creepy outdoor disco. We came out the other side, closer to the building and the ambulance.

Russ and another woman I recognized as one of our employees sat on the back edge of the ambulance, a paramedic working on each of them. Streaks of dark blood ran down the side of Russ' head and dampened the left shoulder of his shirt, but he was upright and talking.

I would have thrown my arms around him if that wouldn't have gotten in the way of his treatment. "What happened?"

"Reverse osmosis machine exploded," Russ said. The paramedic dabbed at Russ' skull, and he grimaced. "I got clipped with some shrapnel. Might have been worse if I hadn't climbed out from under the machine to talk to you right before it happened."

"It would have been worse," Quincey Dornbush said from beside me. "It blew up like a gigantic pressure cooker. He could have been killed."

Heat burned over my face, and my hands went cold. Coincidences happened—my parents exploited that fact all the time to help get their clients acquitted—but in the big things, when it really mattered, I had a theory they were rarer. And it seemed like an awfully big coincidence that our reverse osmosis machine exploded and could have killed the person trying to repair it so soon after our repairman was hit in the head, sending him into a coma.

I caught Elise's glance, but I didn't know her well enough yet to know if she'd come to the same conclusion. Despite her similarities to Mark, she wasn't his twin. He already had one of those in Grant, and even they reacted differently.

I nodded toward the other side of the ambulance. "How many others were hurt?"

"Nancy and I are the worst of it," Russ said. "When the RO machine blew, it knocked over the evaporator and she got splattered with boiling sap."

Two was bad enough. I turned to Quincey. "May I look inside?"

"You can look in the door." He made a firm line with his hand, as if blocking off how far I could go.

"The chief wants the bomb dogs to go through it before we let anyone back in."

Well, at least I knew I wasn't the only one who thought the timeline was suspicious.

My eyes must have gone round or the color must have drained from my face because Quincey patted the air with his hands. "It's a precaution. You know how the chief likes to cross his I's and all that. We don't know the cause of the explosion yet, and given what happened here last week, he wants to be sure."

Elise tapped my elbow. "I'll go to the door with you."

I took it as her signal that she wanted to talk to me privately, so I nodded.

"Not exactly how I'd hoped to get Noah's case classified as an attempted murder," she said as soon as we were far enough away not to be overheard.

It hadn't been mine, either. "Did you look at the name I gave you?"

"Her father's Tony Rathmell. He owns Quantum Mechanics."

That's what I'd been worried about.

We stopped at the door. It hung open. The inside looked like a tornado had touched down. Pieces of the reverse osmosis machine littered the floor, and the evaporator lay on its side. Glass shards and sap were everywhere. The room reeked of charred sap and overheated metal.

This was going to be hard, if not impossible, to recover from this season. Given how expensive the machinery was, I doubted we kept backups hanging around, but I'd ask Russ later to be certain. As soon as the police cleared the building, I'd have to start cleanup with whatever employees agreed to stay and help. I'd hold no ill will against anyone who would rather leave. They'd experienced a trauma.

The big question was whether or not someone had done this on purpose, and why.

"Do you think this was meant for Noah as well?" I asked Elise.

She was staring into the building with a dazed expression like she hadn't expected it to look as bad as it did. "If Noah hadn't been in the hospital, he would have been the one working on anything that malfunctioned?"

I nodded.

She shrugged and one corner of her mouth narrowed. "It'd still be a long shot, wouldn't it? Noah might not have been around when it blew."

True enough, though Russ had been under the machine because it'd been sounding strange. If Noah hadn't already been in the hospital, he would have been the one to do it, and I likely wouldn't have been calling him. "Maybe it was a fluke. Maybe it has nothing to do with Noah's situation at all."

Elise continued to stare into the room rather than looking at me. "Maybe."

# Chapter 13

The paramedics wanted to take Russ to the hospital for a CT scan of his head to rule out internal bleeding. Elise and I backed them up.

Russ crossed his arms over his broad chest. "I should be here to help with cleanup."

I mimicked his stance. "With the mess that's in there, I guarantee we'll still be cleaning up once the doctor clears you."

"Don't make me order you," Elise said.

Russ swiveled his gaze to her, and the look he shot her screamed *traitor*. "Unless my health is a police matter, I'm pretty sure you can't order me to do anything."

Stubborn old man. But Elise had given me an idea. "Don't make me pull rank then. Fifty-one percent, remember?"

Russ lowered his arms and shook his head. "I suppose I deserve that for not treating you like a full partner before." He heaved out a sigh. "I'll go, but you don't go in that place until Quincey says it's safe."

"I promise." I tried to mimic the Scout's Honor sign with my hand, but since I'd never been a girl scout, I wasn't sure I got it right.

I thought I heard Russ mutter *crazy girl*, but the paramedic closed the back door before I could ask him to repeat it.

It was an hour later before the bomb squad said we were good to go. The sky was navy blue and getting darker. Three employees, including Dave from the rental shop when he heard what happened, had volunteered to stay. Nancy, even with her wounds, had wanted to, but the paramedics insisted she go to the hospital as well.

But one employee had quit. With Noah's injury and then the explosion, they weren't comfortable working at Sugarwood anymore. Another girl, one of our teen workers, let me know that her parents would probably insist she quit as well when they found out.

Elise stayed until all the emergency vehicles cleared away. "My shift's over at 6:00. If you wanted, I could ask my mom to stay a bit longer with the kids, and I could come back and lend an extra set of hands. I don't know how to make maple syrup, but I do know how to clean."

My throat closed up. It was no wonder this town and the people in it showed such a loyalty to the Cavanaughs. My parents were feared, respected even. They weren't necessarily liked. If they ever fell from their pedestal, I doubt there'd be many who'd stick around to help them put it back together again.

I didn't want that to be said of me. I wanted to be liked. To be the kind of person who showed up when she was needed. Hopefully Fair Haven could ignore the rumors and give me a chance to prove that's the kind of person I could be.

I gave Elise a shaky smile. "I appreciate it, but I don't want to take you away from your kids. Police officers have to work long enough hours as it is."

She held up her cell phone. "Call me if you change your mind. I'm heading into my days off, so I'll have a little extra time." She headed for her car, but turned back. "And I'll make sure Erik has the name you sent me before I go."

"Could you do one other thing for me?"

She raised an eyebrow.

I might regret this, but it seemed like the right thing to do. Even if Mark and I weren't close anymore, I didn't want him hearing about this second-hand and potentially worrying about Russ. "Could you let Mark know that everyone here is okay? I know he tends to worry."

Elise's smile was one of those knowing ones that always made me want to blow a raspberry at the person giving it. "I can do that," she said.

We'd barely started to clean up when Russ called from the hospital, needing a ride home. I ducked into his house to grab the keys to his truck since my car was still in a ditch down the road.

As I pulled into the hospital parking lot, the headlights flashed across a shuffling figure. The gait reminded me of—

I slammed the brakes a bit too hard, and my body jerked forward. Pain bit through my shoulder again.

The walk reminded me of Tony, but there was no good reason for Tony to be at the hospital. It had to be my imagination playing tricks on me. It'd been a rough day.

Even if it was Tony, he shouldn't be able to get in to see Noah. Erik had said he'd give the nurses a list of approved people. Assuming, of course, a nurse was nearby enough to notice a visitor, which had been my original concern about the plan.

It wouldn't hurt to take a detour up to Noah's room to make sure he was alright.

I bypassed the emergency waiting room where Russ said he'd meet me and took the elevator to Noah's room. Normally I hated elevators. I always envisioned them plummeting to the basement and turning all my bones into goo on impact. When alone, I'd always pick the stairs. But if Tony had done something to Noah, the extra time taking the stairs could cost everything.

When the elevator doors opened, I fast-walked to Noah's room. None of the nurses were at the desk.

*Dear God, please let Noah still be alive.*

I broke into a jog and careened through the door to Noah's room. He lay as still as he had the last time I'd seen him. All the monitors read normal.

I slumped against the door frame. At least no one was around to catch my latest bout of paranoia. I didn't even have proof that Tony had tried to see Noah. He might have injured himself at work or been dropping someone else off. He might know someone else who was in the hospital on an entirely different floor.

I went downstairs and found Russ waiting for me exactly where he said he'd be. "Sorry I'm a couple minutes later than expected. I ducked upstairs to see Noah."

I didn't see any need to tell him I'd gone up because my mind decided to play tricks on me.

"How's the cleanup going?" Russ asked as we headed out for his truck.

"It's going to take a while." That might have been the understatement of all my time here, but the bigger problem was what we'd do once we'd cleaned up the sugar shack. You couldn't crazy glue a reverse osmosis machine back together. "Do we have replacement equipment or any way to get new equipment before the sap stops running?"

Russ lifted a hand to his head like it might be hurting him.

I moved closer in case he got unsteady. Who knew how much blood he'd lost. Head wounds tended to flow like a fountain.

I shuddered and turned my thoughts away. If I kept thinking about blood, I'd be the one who needed steadying. "Did the doctor give you something for the pain?"

Russ produced a bottle of pills. "I'll take one when we're on the way. I need to be able to help tonight."

Like heck he was. "You'll take one because you need to be able to rest."

"No chance we'd get replacement equipment in time." He stuffed the pill bottle back in his pocket. "We should still have our old reverse osmosis machine in the secondary shed, though. How bad was the evaporator damaged?"

I didn't miss the fact that he'd dodged answering my question, which was typical for Russ when he didn't want to argue but didn't intend to go along with whatever someone wanted, either.

And he'd trapped me. I wouldn't know whether the evaporator was just a little dented or if the most essential part had broken off. I also didn't know which of the employees might be able to tell me. "I guess you *will* need to take a look, but then managerial tasks only until you're healed. No cleaning or lifting. Deal?"

The look on his face clearly said *we'll see.* "We can probably get the evaporator fixed, but it'll likely be beyond what I can do. I'll give Tony a call. He used to come by and help us out before we hired Noah full-time."

I clambered up into the driver's seat. What reason—that he'd believe—could I give for having someone other than Tony come out? If he had the most experience apart from Noah with our machinery, he was the obvious choice. Technically he couldn't do any more damage. Noah was in the hospital, not at Sugarwood, and if he'd sabotaged the equipment to hurt Noah, he'd have no reason to tamper with it again.

Maybe my problem was that I simply didn't trust him right now, and it would be awkward being around him knowing what I knew about his daughter and Noah.

All of that led into our bigger problem—we needed someone we could depend on to keep our machinery running. As weird as he was, Oliver must be a good mechanic or Tony wouldn't have hired him. Erik told me Tony only hired the best. "If Noah doesn't recover, we can't expect Tony to drop his real business at a moment's notice to help us. I was thinking maybe we should invite Oliver. I got the impression that he'd be open to leaving Quantum Mechanics for the right job."

Russ squished up half of his mouth. "Ollie's a nice enough guy, but he's not the best with people. He'd make a terrible tour guide."

"He doesn't need to do everything Noah did. I can give the tours myself, or we can see if any of our other employees might like the position. Noah said the tips were excellent."

Russ gave a slow nod as if he were afraid of making his headache worse. "Something to consider. I guess there's no harm in asking Oliver to come along this time at least. Get a sense of how he works, and the repairs should go faster. I don't know what else might have been damaged in the blast yet."

We came around the bend in the drive that led to the sugar shack. Cars lined the shoulders.

My whole body suddenly felt encased in concrete. The number of cars had more than doubled. Even if a few of the employees changed their minds and came back, there shouldn't have been this many.

Unless something else had gone wrong.

# Chapter 14

I parked Russ' truck in the first available space, jumped out, and sprinted toward the building, praying the whole way.

One step inside the door, I skidded to a stop. Dave and the other employees who'd been here when I left were still here, but they'd been joined by people who should have had no reason to be here.

Dana from my Lost Pets group, her baby strapped on her back in one of those carriers that reminded me of a Native American papoose board. Mandy, the owner of The Sunburnt Arms where I'd stayed for the first weeks I was in Fair Haven. Jesse, the owner of The Burnt Toast Café, whose daughter I'd helped with her application to law school.

Alongside them were a few people I didn't know.

And Mark and Elise, even though I'd told her she didn't need to come back.

Despite all the rumors, despite all the stupid things I'd done, it seemed like more people cared about me and Russ and Sugarwood than I'd realized. This sense of community, the connectedness between all of us, was something I couldn't have found in the city. I'd been afraid that, thanks to the rumors, I wouldn't find it here either. Thank God I'd been wrong.

Elise must have spotted me standing by the door. She headed in my direction, one of those rare smiles that showed her Cavanaugh dimples on her face.

"The mess looked too big for a few people if you want to be up and running in time to still make syrup this season." Elise shrugged. "So Mark and I made a few calls. Quincey's on the night shift, but Erik's going to come by when he gets off duty if you still need him."

I was one breath away from busting into tears when Russ huffed in the door behind me.

He let slip a curse word. "Where did all these people come from?"

"Apparently," I linked my arm through his, "all these people are addicted to our syrup, and they're afraid they won't get their fix."

Russ reached up a hand as though he intended to ruffle his hair, but his fingers hit the bandage and he settled for scratching at it instead. "I'll take a look at the evaporator and then make a call about repairs."

In the meantime, I should make sure the path was clear to our other reverse osmosis machine. We'd want to move it into the sugar shack while we still had strong backs to help us. "Where do I find the keys to the secondary shed?"

"You probably have one on Stan's old keyring." Russ unclipped the key chain from his belt and handed it to me. "We only had the three copies—mine, Stan's, and Noah's. Too much expensive equipment to have extras floating around."

By the time I made sure a big enough path was cleared to the old reverse osmosis machine and returned to the sugar shack, Tony was bent over the evaporator and legs that I assumed belonged to Oliver stuck out from underneath.

I stopped near the protruding legs. "I appreciate you both coming out."

Tony grunted, his nose a fraction of an inch from a piece of the machine I couldn't hope to identify.

"Everything looks good down here." Oliver worm-crawled out from underneath. "I'll make sure the other evaporators are okay."

I followed after him. Noah had his keys on him when he was attacked—I remembered them gouging into my leg when I tried to help him—and his belongings must have gone somewhere once he got to the hospital. Oliver might have them or might know where they were, and we should get the keys back rather than allowing them to float around in the wild.

"Do you know what happened to Noah's belong-ings? We need to get his keys back."

Oliver blink-blinked at me. "They're probably still at the hospital. No one gave me anything."

I'd have to check tomorrow, assuming I could get there. My first task would be to have my car towed out of the ditch and to Quantum Mechanics. As much as Tony's involvement in Noah's situation was questiona-ble, his was still the shop I trusted since they'd taken care of me the last two times. Besides, Tony would have no reason to hurt me.

A hand rested on my shoulder from behind me. From the size, I knew it was a man's, and from the an-gle, it couldn't be Russ. With Erik not here, that left only one man who would touch me.

From the lewd smirk on Oliver's face as he turned away, my expression must have telegraphed how I felt about the person the hand belonged to.

I shifted around, breaking the contact. As suspect-ed, Mark stood behind me.

I knew I should thank him for coming, but what I really wanted to do was fall into his arms for a hug. Since my Uncle Stan moved to Michigan and then passed away, there'd been a deficit of hugs in my life. Even when I'd been dating someone, our embraces wouldn't have been classified as the kind of tell-me-everything's-going-to-be-alright type of hug I needed now.

Concern flickered across Mark's face. How long had I been staring wordlessly at his chest?

"Are you okay?" he asked.

A crazy laugh bubbled up inside me. I held it back. If I started talking about how not okay I was, how afraid I was that I was going to lose Sugarwood, I might cry right here in front of everyone, and I was too much my father's daughter to ever do that. "I'll be better once we get this mess cleaned up."

Mark shook his head. "I meant are you hurt. Elise said you ran your car into a ditch because you were on the phone with Russ when it happened."

Oh. Right. Doctor. He was asking after my physical health. "My shoulder aches a little, but it still works, and it's starting to feel better already." I scrubbed my teeth over the corner of my upper lip. "Thanks for asking."

Mark started to turn away, then stopped. "I know Erik's busy right now, and Russ shouldn't drive for a few days. If you'll let me, I'll make sure your car gets to Quantum Mechanics."

A lump clogged my throat, so I answered with a nod. Mark headed back to where Elise had wheeled in a wheelbarrow and was shoveling up bits of glass and metal.

I headed over to the pile of work gloves someone had left on a card table set up in the corner and put my face to the wall for a minute. It was the best chance I'd have at privacy and to get control of my emotions for hours.

Unless Mark Cavanaugh turned from Dr. Jekyll into Mr. Hyde, my chances of falling out of love with him seemed about as good as an eighty-degree day in a Michigan December.

Since Russ wasn't supposed to be driving anywhere for a couple of days in case his head wound made him dizzy, he gave me free access to his truck. Unfortunately, with getting everything back up and running, I didn't have time to go by the hospital for nearly a week.

Knowing the keys were out there unprotected was like having a cracked lip. It made it difficult for me to do even the normal tasks without distraction. I called the hospital and asked them to take Noah's belongings out of the cubby in his room and set them behind their desk. Presumably, no one would think to hunt through the storage cubbies of comatose patients—most next of kin would have taken the items home—and even if someone did find them, they'd need to figure out where to use them. But I still hated them out there unprotected. I'd had too many people invade my "home" to be comfortable with possibly providing them with easy access to everywhere on Sugarwood. At least my house keys weren't included. The only one who had a key to my house other than me was Russ.

Once again, no one even stopped to ask my name as I entered Noah's room. The nurses were too busy to be expected to also guard Noah. Though, by now, if no one had come to finish what they started, I had to assume that they were satisfied with putting him into a coma. According to Oliver, the doctors had given up hope that he'd ever wake up.

After stopping in to see Noah, I waited for a nurse and asked after Noah's belongings. The keys were at the top of the plastic bag that someone had put his belongings in to. The keys technically belonged to Sugarwood, so I felt entitled to take those with me, but I left the rest behind for Oliver to pick up if he wanted.

I was leaving the hospital when Elise's name flashed across my phone.

"I'm headed to interview Stacey Rathmell, and I was hoping you'd ride along. Mark says you're great at reading people. You've probably noticed that I'm not. I was sure when I arrived at the scene of Noah's attack that you'd done it." Her tone of voice had that self-deprecating, *I'm going to laugh at my failings so that at least we can laugh together* quality to it.

Maybe staying up all night, scrubbing sap off of concrete floors, bonded people. Or maybe I was lonelier here than I wanted to admit. Whatever the reason, I'd almost considered calling up Elise to chat a couple days ago. Her admission of her weakness as an interrogator suggested that we might be able to be friends yet.

*Either that*, the pernicious little voice in my head whispered, *or she's trying to get you to let your guard down so that she can trick you into admitting you did do it.*

This time I was ninety-nine percent certain that my paranoid self was wrong.

I climbed into Russ' truck and turned it on for the heater, but I didn't leave the parking lot since his truck wasn't Bluetooth-equipped.

My first reaction was to say *of course!* to Elise's suggestion, but Erik's concerns about the scrutiny the department was under lingered in my mind.

"If you take me along, won't that get you into trouble?"

"I got Erik to sign off on it as long as you're along as potential council should Stacey request it."

No one could argue with that. I glanced down at my jeans and running shoes. If I was going to be along as a lawyer, I needed to look the part.

Since it might call my validity as a lawyer into question if I showed up in Russ' mud-spattered truck, I'd probably need a ride there as well.

"I'm out right now, and I'll need to change. Can you meet me at Sugarwood in fifteen minutes?"

# Chapter 15

Stacey Rathmell lived at home with her parents, and their house turned out to be in a subdivision not far from Quantum Mechanics. The house was a Cape Cod-style with dormered windows on the second floor, green shutters, and a steeply sloping roof perfect for winters with heavy snow. The first word that came to my mind was *unpretentious*. It was how I would have described Tony as well, so I suppose it fit.

Elise knocked on the door, and Stacey answered. She looked almost identical to the way she had in the picture. That suggested they might have been recent rather than taken a couple of years ago the way we'd assumed. People changed a lot in their teens, so it wasn't likely she'd look the same now as she had at fifteen.

Or maybe I was reaching because I didn't want Noah to have been guilty of what he'd been accused of. We might not have been close, but I'd liked him, and I didn't want to like him if he'd been preying on underage girls.

Stacey's gaze zipped over Elise's uniform and then hopped to me. She dropped the backpack she'd been holding to the ground. "Did something happen to one of my parents?"

Elise showed her badge, even though her uniform made it clear she was the police. "We're here to talk to you about Noah Miller."

Stacey rocked back and forth as though she were trying to decide between inviting us in and slamming the door in our face. It was an odd reaction.

She slung her backpack over her shoulder. "I was on my way to class, actually."

Elise had filled me in on the way on the little she'd found out about Stacey. Other than her ill-fated appearance in the court records surrounding Noah's statutory rape charge, she must have kept her head down to stay so far out of the everybody-knows-everybody rumor mill of Fair Haven. From what Elise told me, Stacey'd been the model child and now was going to school for automotive technology, with the intent of taking over her father's business when he retired. Other than the fact that she'd once been a girl scout, the gossip puddle ran shallow. I had more of a reputation after a few months than Stacey Rathmell did after living here her whole life.

It spoke to how careful Tony and his wife must have been in protecting their children. That knowledge kept me from dismissing entirely the idea that Tony had somehow been involved in Noah's attack.

"We won't take up too much of your time," Elise said, "but it is important that we talk to you."

Stacey stepped back out of the doorway, the only invitation she gave for us to enter. She didn't make the usual requests that a reticent adult might have about whether we had a warrant or whether answering our questions was mandatory. It was looking like she wouldn't even question who I was or why I was there.

Elise entered, and I followed.

Stacey had that same way of avoiding eye contact that Tony had. It seemed contrary to the pictures where she'd either been looking straight into the camera or straight at Noah.

Stacey showed us to the living room, but she stayed standing. "I don't know how much help I can be." Her gaze shifted from side to side, and she twisted a lock of hair around her finger.

Elise didn't really need me. The girl was a terrible liar. Based on her body language tells when she said that, she felt like she had a lot to say about Noah.

"You've heard about what happened to Noah?" Elise asked. She'd taken a seat on the couch, which was a bit of a miscalculation. Since she was asking the questions, she should have stayed upright so she didn't have to look up at Stacey. I should have been the one to sit, indicating that we were going to stay until we'd had our questions answered.

But Elise had admitted that she wasn't good at this. It wasn't like anyone was born knowing how to read and manipulate others. I'd learned, probably much too young.

"I heard," Stacey said. She'd stopped twisting her hair, but held one hand in the other. "I tried to go see him, but there was some sort of list, and I wasn't on it."

I barely kept myself from rolling my eyes. That was just great. The nurses managed to keep the one person I was pretty sure hadn't hurt Noah from seeing him.

Elise should follow that up with a question about why she'd gone to see Noah. I glanced in her direction. Was I supposed to simply listen and observe here or was I allowed to ask questions as well?

Elise pulled out a notebook and a pen. "We believe that what happened to Noah wasn't an accident."

Stacey turned a pasty green. "You think someone hurt him on purpose?"

Only my parents' years of drilled in training prevented me from slumping. Way to give away the whole sack of potatoes, Elise. That information should have been held back until the end.

Hopefully Elise would forgive me, but I had to jump in or this whole visit could be a waste. "We're not sure yet. We're trying to find out a bit more about Noah that might help us understand what he was like."

I avoided saying if anyone had a reason to hurt him. People tended to shut down if they thought you might be implying that they or their loved ones had something to do with a crime.

"Your name came up in connection to Noah," I said.

A leading statement rather than a question. When a person was already nervous, the way Stacey was, they'd often be inclined to ramble if given a bit of a nudge.

She sat in the nearest chair. "He used to work for my dad."

Smart girl. She'd probably come up with that strategy for answering questions about Noah the last time police officers had come around asking about him. Unfortunately for us.

"You won't get in trouble if you tell us what happened, and neither will Noah." Elise tucked her pen inside her notebook as if to imply that she wouldn't even take notes. "We're only investigating his potential attack, not what he personally might have done in the past."

If we'd been alone, I would have high-fived her. Interviewing might not have come naturally to her, but it looked like she'd be a quick study with some more practice.

Stacey's face set into hard lines from her eyebrows to her lips. "If you knew enough to find me, then you know what I told the police when they asked three years ago. Noah never did anything he shouldn't have, and my dad didn't know what he was talking about when he said Noah did."

There was a fierceness to her response, like you only see in people who're defending someone they care about deeply from an unwarranted attack. That, combined with how obviously uncomfortable she'd been when she tried to lie to us before, made me believe her. But there were still the pictures to explain.

I pulled a photo that I'd hung on to out of my purse and turned it toward Stacey. It was one of the ones that showed Noah and Stacey kissing.

Stacey gave the cross-armed shrug that teenagers seemed to be masters of. "So? That was taken after I turned eighteen. We're two consenting adults. If you don't believe me, you can check on when I got the earrings I'm wearing. They were a gift from my parents at my last birthday."

Elise's shoulders went tight. It was one of her tells. She didn't know where to take this next.

I looked down at the photo long enough that I knew it would make Stacey uncomfortable.

Finally I met her gaze and tapped a finger on the edge of the picture. "You can see how this makes it look, though. Like maybe this started before your birthday."

"I could say you can't prove that, but I'm tired of people trying to trick me into admitting something that isn't true." She smacked a palm into the arm of her chair. "Noah didn't touch me while I was under-age." She punctuated each word with another slap, then her hand stilled. "I wanted him to, but he said he wanted to do things right. We'd wait, and if we still wanted to be together once I turned eighteen, then no one could stop us."

The words I should say fled from my mind. On one hand, Noah had done the right thing. On the other hand, Noah was old enough to be her dad. Could a relationship with such a big age gap be genuine, with no ulterior motives?

Stacey scowled at me. "You think I don't know what that look on your face means. I've seen it on every adult who's talked to me about this."

I schooled my features so the skepticism I was feeling didn't show through. She'd been probed about their relationship so much that she'd be on the defensive with almost anything I asked, and we'd end up no further ahead about whether or not Tony might have decided to hurt Noah after all these years. I needed to find a way to disarm her. What might she actually *want* to talk about?

"Maybe if you told us a little more about how this started?" I said. "What attracted you two to each other?"

Stacey leaned back into her chair, pulled one knee up to her torso, and hugged it to her. She looked more like a vulnerable child than a rebellious teenager. "No one's ever asked me that before." Her voice was soft.

"Even now, no one cares *why* we want to be together. They only care about our age difference."

"I care," Elise said. "We both do."

Stacey licked her lips. "It's not easy, you know. Going through high school when you're not one of the popular girls. My parents had rules for what I could wear and the kind of parties I could go to. It didn't make me very popular. And I had nothing in common with all the kids who might have been willing to be my friends. I liked to go to my dad's shop on the weekends and after school and learn about cars." Her gaze slid to the photo. "That's how I met Noah."

I moved to the edge of my seat and leaned forward to indicate interest. It wasn't hard. I was interested.

"Noah was always willing to show me stuff. Not all the guys there wanted a teenage girl hanging around and asking questions. Noah and I started talking about cars and eventually about other things. Turned out we had more in common than I had with any of the guys at school."

"So why did your dad think something inappropriate was happening?" Elise prompted.

"He said Noah was flirting with me, and he told me he didn't want me spending time with him anymore. I'd sneak into the shop nights when I knew Noah'd be working late alone, and one time my dad caught me there. We weren't doing anything, but he assumed we had been and he went to the police."

One of the puzzle pieces slid into place in my mind. "And he told everyone that he'd fired Noah for stealing because he didn't want the real reason getting out?"

Stacey nodded. "It wasn't fair. But Noah said we just had to be patient. We had our first kiss the day after I turned eighteen." Her voice was so wet with tears that I almost couldn't understand the end of what she'd said.

I caught the gist. They'd waited three years to become a couple, only for Noah to end up in a coma shortly after.

And now I knew how to get to the question we really wanted to know, but doing it made me feel a bit like I was covered in sludge and smelled like it, too. "How do your parents feel about your relationship with Noah?"

"My dad freaked out when I told him Noah and I were engaged. He thought it proved that Noah had pressured me into sleeping with him three years ago and that we'd been meeting secretly ever since. He said Noah only wanted my help to pay off his gambling debt." She swiped the back of her hand across her cheek. "I offered to help Noah, we even argued about it, and he refused. It wasn't about money."

I studiously kept my gaze from snaking to Elise. We'd wondered why now, after three years, the father of the girl Noah'd been accused of molesting would seek revenge. Stacey'd given us a possible answer. That same man wanted to marry his daughter, maybe use her to ease the burden of his gambling debt. Given how devoted to Noah Stacey seemed and how long they'd waited to be together, it wasn't likely they'd be dissuaded either.

But would Tony have tried to kill Noah over it? Maybe he came to Sugarwood to talk to him, man to man, and when Noah refused to give Stacey up, Tony's anger got the best of him.

Elise was on her feet. "Thanks for helping us better understand the situation. I'll make sure you're put on the list of people who're allowed access to Noah."

Elise handed her a business card and asked her to call if she thought of anyone who might have wanted to hurt Noah. It was sneakier than I would have expected from Elise. We had an answer from Stacey already for who had a motive to hurt Noah, but giving her the card and leaving the idea hanging meant Stacey might volunteer another name as well. For the sake of Tony's whole family and Noah, I still wanted to hope someone else had done this.

Outside, the snow flurries of earlier had become thumbnail-sized wet flakes. They drenched my hair.

When we climbed back into the car, Elise and I sat in silence for almost a minute. All I could think was that Stacey was really going to hate us if we ended up proving that her father tried to kill her fiancé. We'd been the first people who'd seemed to believe her about Noah, and we were secretly using her.

As much as I knew we were trying to work toward the greater good, and that people couldn't be allowed to go around killing each other simply because they didn't want someone marrying their daughter, I still wished I wasn't involved in this case anymore. I didn't need to be. This was a choice I'd made. Glutton for punishment, my Uncle Stan would have said.

"I always expect to feel better when a strong lead comes along," I said. "But so far I've ended up feeling like the Grinch stealing Christmas."

"I probably shouldn't tell you this," Elise smoothed her hands over her already-smooth hair, "but this is my first investigation. Erik only let me keep going with it because I'm the one who believed it wasn't an accident from the start."

I'd wondered. Elise seemed very inexperienced with investigating to have been given the lead on this case now that it was a case.

"I've known Tony a long time," she said. "I don't want it to be him."

That was a sentiment I could echo. At least in Uncle Stan's murder, I'd been wrong about it being Russ. In the other cases I'd been involved in, it hadn't turned out as well.

"One of the reasons I quit my job as a criminal defense attorney was that I didn't want to defend people who were guilty. Now I keep stumbling onto cases where the people I want to be innocent are guilty, and part of me actually wants to defend them."

"Just because Tony had a motive doesn't mean he did it." Elise started the car. The windshield wipers squeaked like wet sneakers on a tile floor. "We'll still need to see if he has an alibi for the time of the attack. And we don't have the weapon yet, either. Did you check your barn to see if there was blood on anything outside the stall?"

I nodded. "I figured that whatever the attacker used they either brought with them or took with them afterward. I didn't think to look for anything that might be missing and would fit the type of wound Mark described."

Elise dug at the braiding on her steering wheel with her pinky finger nail. "Shaped like a miniature horseshoe."

If we assumed Tony was the assailant, then his weapon of choice might have been a tool. "Is there a tool that would make that shape?"

"A wrench, maybe. If it was swung sideways like a baseball bat. But Mark would know better." She slid her gaze sideways toward me and a smile played at the corner of her lips. "Should I call him and ask?"

Elise seemed to have the same naiveté about social interactions as Mark did, so she must have thought teasing me about a man I cared for and couldn't have would help me get over him. I couldn't come up with any other reason. I should tell her to call after she dropped me off, but that felt more like something a high schooler would do than a grown woman.

And I had to admit—I missed hearing Mark's voice. "Might as well."

My attempt at an it's-all-the-same-to-me tone failed. Miserably.

Elise stuck an ear bud into her ear, and asked me to dial the number on her phone so she could keep her attention on driving. The falling snow had already created a slick sheet on the road.

I put Mark's number in and tapped the green phone icon to dial.

"Grant?" Elise said. "What are you doing with—" She sucked in a breath so sharp she could have swallowed her tongue, and her face went slack. She listened for a minute. "No, I'm coming. I don't care."

My mouth dried up, and it felt like a hand reached into my chest and squeezed my heart. There was only one reason Grant would have Mark's phone, and that Elise would go to wherever they were even though she was supposed to be working. Something had happened to Mark.

# Chapter 16

Elise seemed to have forgotten I was in the car with her. She disconnected the call with Grant and dialed another number on her phone.

"I need to take a family care day," she said to whoever was on the other end. "No, it's Mark. I'm heading to the hospital now..."

The other person must have asked her if she was alone or needed something because she jerked slightly and her gaze shifted to me. "I'll be okay. Nicole's still with me. We'll stay together. I'll call to tell you how he is when I know more."

She disconnected the call, yanked the ear bud from her ear, and gripped the steering wheel. The car picked up speed, faster than I would have felt safe to drive in the snow, but Elise was a Northerner, plus she'd likely had training in driving in adverse weather conditions.

I wasn't going to complain. My heart beat so hard and fast I could barely breathe, and Elise's driving would get us to the hospital faster. As long as we were heading to the hospital, there had to still be hope. He was alive, and doctors were taking care of him.

The part of me that always seemed more scared little girl than grown-up woman wanted to cover her ears and hum. If I didn't hear what had happened, it couldn't possibly be true.

The rest of me wanted the worst up-front, as soon as possible. You couldn't deal with the unknown. "What happened?"

Elise seemed to be struggling to swallow. The muscles in her jawline tensed and her throat worked. "Grant's not sure exactly what caused it, but Mark slammed into the back of a semi. They don't know how bad it is yet. They're waiting for a doctor to come talk to them, but they're not able to see him so..."

She trailed off as if she didn't know how to finish the thought.

She didn't have to. I knew. If they weren't allowed to see him, it meant he was either in surgery or the doctors were working hard to stabilize him and they didn't want panicky family members in the way.

I should tell her that I'd call a cab when we got to the hospital because they didn't need a non-family member hanging around. (Did Fair Haven even have a cab service?) Though it sounded like she wanted me to stay with her even though I didn't belong.

I could do that. I could be her support system for as long as she needed it.

My throat closed. I could even handle meeting Mark's wife and seeing them together if Elise needed me. I'd been pining for a friend and missing Ahanti despite our frequent phone conversations. If I had a chance at a friendship with Elise, I had to be willing to *suck it up, buttercup* and be her friend when she needed it most, regardless of what it cost me.

"Their parents are snow birds," Elise said out of nowhere. "They spend the winter in Florida. I hope Grant thought to call them. I'll have to call my parents once we know more."

Her thoughts had to be as much of a jumble as mine. *Focus, Nicole. One of you needs to stay focused.* "Did Grant say where to meet him?"

"Megan's going to be waiting for us out front."

That could be either Grant's wife or Mark's wife. And I was *not* asking.

Elise got us safely to the hospital parking lot and led the way to the emergency room doors. I slipped along behind her in my now totally inappropriate heels. They'd made sense when I was posing as a lawyer, though Stacey'd never even asked who I was. Now they were a liability. I couldn't support Elise if I fell and broke my arm. I shuffled my feet instead of picking them up off the ground.

The woman who met us at the door didn't look anything like the blonde in the photographs above Mark's fireplace.

Meagan Cavanaugh was closer to my short stature than to Elise's height and had a heavy dash of freckles across her nose and cheeks. Her red-brown hair was pulled back into a ponytail. She reminded me a bit of a buxom pixie.

Elise quickly made introductions, and Meagan didn't even question my presence with her body language or a sidelong glance. It felt like she should have. I wasn't family. And surely she'd heard the rumors about me the same as Elise had. The woman had no reason to welcome or accept me.

I tottered along behind them inside, the floors nearly more slick than the pavement had been. Finally I yanked my shoes off and walked barefoot.

A doctor was already talking to Grant as we turned the final corner. There was an openness to Grant's posture, hands loose at his sides and a relaxed curve to his knees.

I grabbed Elise's sleeve. "He's going to be okay."

Elise frowned. "How do you know?"

"The way Grant's standing. It says *thank God* rather than *I'm bracing myself.*"

She looked at Grant and then back to me. "He just looks like he's standing there to me."

Grant turned to us with a smile. I blinked twice before my brain fully registered that it was Grant and not Mark. Grant didn't have the same dimples or the same premature grey at his temples, but they were otherwise identical.

Meagan walked straight into his arms, and a tiny bead of jealousy formed in my heart. Not over Grant, but over what they had. I kicked it back into the dark corner it came from. Now wasn't the time.

"How is he?" Elise asked.

"Waking up. They had to put him under because the collision broke his wrist and they needed to set it. But other than that, some bad bruises, and a fractured nose, the doctor said he's going to be fine, and we can see him. He gave me the room number."

They headed down the hall, and I hung back. Elise was safe with family. It might be time for me to bow out gracefully before I had to come face to face with Mrs. Mark Cavanaugh.

Elise turned back and quirked her eyebrow as if to say *what are you doing?*

Or I could simply go, say hello, and set my mind at ease that he was going to be okay. Then I'd leave before any other family arrived.

Mark's room wasn't on the same floor as Noah's, which made me feel even better. They'd placed Mark on the short-term-stay floor.

He looked the way I'd have imagined someone who'd just been in a car accident would look. His nose and around his eyes shone with the trademark black-purple of a fresh bruise. He'd been propped up slightly, and his arm lay in a sling across his chest. But his eyes were open, and he almost managed a smile as we all filed in.

I knew the moment he caught sight of me because his forehead got all crinkly the way it did when he was confused.

"They gave me too many drugs," Mark said. "I see Nicole."

Elise snort-laughed beside me, and I chewed on the inside of my cheek. What did it say that he thought I'd be his hallucination?

"You do have the same tolerance for medication as a five year old, but it's not the drugs," Grant said with a shake of his head. "That's the real Nicole."

Elise smirked. "Can't you tell from the smeared mascara? If you were hallucinating her, she'd probably look less like a snow-drenched kitten and more like a runway model."

The words hit me like a slap, but then I saw it. This was how Cavanaughs interacted with each other. They teased. Elise wasn't being mean. She was treating me like part of her family.

I swiped my fingers under my eyes, which probably only made the mess worse. I hadn't counted on slushy snow when I got ready this morning. I definitely hadn't planned on seeing Mark. But if they expected me to take it, I was going to give it to. "I wanted to match

Mark so he wouldn't feel so bad about those raccoon bruises."

Mark's dimples popped out, and he cringed. "Maybe don't make me laugh. My whole face feels a bit like I offered to be a punching bag for a prize fighter." His lips twitched again, but he held the smile in check. "I'm just sorry I won't have a scar. I hear chicks dig those."

He looked straight at me, and heat flamed up into my cheeks. I definitely needed to make my exit.

Meagan rolled her eyes. "Chicks dig those? I think maybe they did give you too many drugs."

"Probably," Mark said. "Even if I'm not hallucinating Nikki, I feel like my words are taking a long time to reach my mouth."

Elise ribbed him about how that might help him stick his foot in his mouth less often, and I stepped backward toward the door. An ache was building around my heart that was threatening to cut off my air supply. I couldn't stay here anymore. Mark was fine, and Elise was fine. I really needed to go. Watching them all was like letting a dehydrated person lick the perspiration off a cup of cold water. I loved Mark, but I would have also loved to be a part of a family like this, and I was pretty sure envy was one of the seven big sins. I definitely envied Mark's wife—not just Mark, but his family as well.

I waved at them. "I wanted to know you were okay, but I should probably go now. The room's small, and I don't want to be in the way when your wife gets here."

The silence that fell made me feel like I'd shouted the F-word in church.

# Chapter 17

I couldn't read the expression on Mark's face. It was almost like he was trying to decide if I'd actually said what I'd said or if the meds were messing with his mind.

Crap. What had I stepped in now? Were they separated? Maybe they were separated and she wasn't going to come and it was a painful topic for Mark.

I looked over at Meagan and Grant, who looked like I'd poured a bucket of ice cubes over him, then swiveled my gaze to Elise. Why was no one saying anything?

I moved back another step, and Elise lunged forward and grabbed my wrist. "Nicole, wait. Did you not know Mark's a widower? His wife died four years ago."

My shoes slipped from my fingers and hit the floor with a double whap.

The pictures on the fireplace mantel but no women's shoes in his entryway. The ring on his finger but no wife at church with him. How he didn't seem like a man who'd cheat on his spouse but still seemed attracted to me and unconcerned by it. All the little inconsistencies crashed into me and made sense.

And all the dirty looks people had given me when we were together, the ones I'd assumed had been because he was married, must have been because of the rumors. They thought I was going to break the heart of Fair Haven's cherished son. In a way, I had.

I reached out a hand for the wall and hung on. I'd thought I knew the situation, but I'd assumed. I'd never asked him bluntly about his wife.

My face was so hot now that I thought I might cry. They must think I was an idiot. And I'd hurt Mark and myself. And dear God, what if he didn't want to date me anyway?

"I think we should go grab a cup of coffee," Meagan said.

Grant took her hand. "Yup. Mark, we'll come back and find out what you need us to bring for you when we're done."

Elise maneuvered me around and pushed me down into the chair by Mark's bedside. "I'm going with them, and you're staying here."

Then I was left staring at Mark, my face so hot you could have roasted marshmallows over it and seriously considering whether you could make yourself invisible if you wished for it hard enough. I dropped my gaze to my bare feet and tried to memorize the pattern on the floor. I had no idea what to say now or where to start, though everyone clearly thought we needed to have a conversation.

The hospital bed creaked as though Mark were shifting position to get a better look at me. "I need to hear you say it." His voice was quiet. "Did you think I was married?"

I nodded, then realized that still wasn't saying it. "That's what I thought. You were wearing a wedding ring." It sounded so naïve now. I'd skipped over an obvious possibility because of my emotional baggage thanks to Peter. "I know people who've lost a spouse often do that, but I've—my last boyfriend turned out to be married, and when I see a ring..."

Great. Now I was rambling like a crazy person.

And Mark wasn't saying anything.

I forced myself to look up. He was grinning, despite his battered face.

"It's not funny," I said, but the pout in my voice was mostly faked. *He isn't married*, kept zipping around in my head, distracting me from everything else. *He isn't married and he doesn't look angry.*

He didn't even attempt to corral his smile. "It's not funny. It might be in hindsight though."

In hindsight, like when we told it ten years down the road? Like one of the stories couples told when they had guests over for dinner?

His expression sobered. "I thought you were dating Erik, but Elise said you're not. Was she right?"

"We had two dates months ago. Now he's just a friend."

Before I could process what was happening, Mark was pulling suction cups off. The machine he'd been connected to wailed.

I stood up. "What are you doing?"

He swung his feet off the bed, a determined look on his face. "I'm going to kiss you."

My stomach flipped over at the same time as he tried to stand and his legs gave out. I leaped forward and helped him lower back to the bed. "You're crazy, you know that."

"It's the drugs."

"It's not."

"No, it's not." He leaned his head back on the pillow, his face only a shade or two pinker than the pillow cover now. "Might have too much sedative in my system to walk yet."

I dragged the chair over next to him. "It looks that way."

I settled in beside him, and he sat up a bit. He stretched his good hand up to my cheek and ran his thumb across my cheekbone, where I probably still had mascara smeared. Tingles shot out from every spot his hand touched. I'd had dreams in the past where Mark's wife disappeared. Part of me wondered if I wasn't asleep now. My brain was still struggling to process the fact that Mark was single and all that meant for us.

"I'd still like to kiss you though," he said.

My heart beat fast enough that it almost hurt in my chest. He couldn't walk. What if he wasn't thinking clearly either? "Are you sure that's not the drugs talking?"

"Very sure."

His slid his hand around to the back of my neck and drew me toward him.

"What's going on in here?!"

I jerked back and Mark dropped his hand.

A middle-aged nurse in bright purple scrubs hustled over to the still beeping machines. "What did you do to these?" She scowled at me as though I'd been the one to rip them off.

I gave her my best *who me?* look because I was having too hard a time not laughing to do anything else. My silly grin probably only made me look extra guilty.

The sedative and pain killers they'd given Mark might have loosened his inhibitions a bit, but he still seemed to have enough good sense to look mollified and lay still while the nurse reconnected the sensors.

"Now try to leave them in place," the nurse said. "We need to monitor you a little longer to make sure you don't go into delayed shock."

With one more stern look at us both, she left.

"I think she saw us," I mocked whispered.

He met my gaze, and his face was serious. "I don't care who sees us."

Very few of my past relationships had lasted long enough to require a definition, but this time I wanted one from the start. I didn't want to risk any more misunderstandings. We lost enough time due to that already.

And yet as I went to ask, I felt a little like a clingy teenager. It was stupid. This was Mark. I shouldn't have to ask. But a small part of me was still afraid, afraid that I'd disappoint him like I'd done so many others, and that if he knew what I was truly like and all my flaws, he wouldn't want to be with me.

He linked his fingers with mine, my mascara smeared over both our hands. Maybe he did see me as I was, my best and my worst.

He squeezed my hand. "What's wrong?"

I wasn't good at being vulnerable. I never had been. Vulnerability and weakness were the same things in my parents' eyes. But Mark was the first man I'd ever met who I wanted as both a best friend and a romantic partner. I had to imagine that combination didn't come around often.

"We've had a lot of misunderstandings, and so could you...could we be clear about what this is?" I lifted our linked hands.

He brought our hands to his lips and kissed my knuckles. A shiver shot straight down my arm and into my stomach.

"I don't want you dating anyone else. I'm sorry I didn't tell you that earlier and that I didn't make sure you knew about Laura."

Her name had been Laura. It was a pretty name. And now that I knew she was a love he'd lost, I wasn't jealous anymore. The ring he still wore spoke to how deeply he could love.

I did want to know exactly what had happened, though. "How did she die?"

"I guess I owe you the story." Mark's Adam's apple bobbed. "I've never had to tell anyone before. Everyone here knows."

The pain that etched his face was so deep I almost regretted asking, but it was the kind of thing I needed to know if we wanted a chance at a future. He'd loved her. Their history would always color our relationship in some way.

"You saw the picture on the mantel," he said.

There'd been more than one, but he must be talking about the picture of him with a pregnant woman. The other photo had been of their wedding day.

"We were living in New York at the time, and I had the privilege of working as part of a team that was trying to develop more sensitive testing procedures for poisons and toxins in the body. She was only seven-and-a-half months along, so we thought it would be safe for me to go out of town to lecture at a convention."

Now that I'd passed the point of no return and saw what was coming, I didn't want to hear anymore. Mark didn't have a child, so she must have lost the baby.

"The baby shifted and the umbilical cord wrapped around her neck. The doctors did an emergency C-section. They managed to save Laura, but not our little girl."

His hand held onto mine so tightly my fingers ached, but I held still.

"Laura blamed me. She thought if I'd been there, I would have been able to save them both."

It was ridiculous. Mark wasn't a pediatric specialist. He dealt with dead bodies, not live ones. And he wouldn't have been allowed to practice on his own wife anyway.

I opened my mouth to say all that, but the look on Mark's face stopped me. The lines around his eyes were tense and carried right down into his jaw bone. He knew all those things. Knew them and yet still struggled to accept them because someone he loved had told him otherwise.

If I said anything to try to console him, it could come out as attacking her. I didn't want to start our relationship that way. "I'm so sorry."

He sucked in a breath. "I quit my job, and was thankfully able to get a position in Fair Haven, where we both grew up. I was hoping bringing her home would help, but her depression got worse and she refused help. One day I came home and found she'd overdosed on sleeping pills."

I slumped back in my chair.

"I didn't want to believe she'd killed herself. I wanted it investigated as a crime, but..." He shook his head. "It wasn't like Stan's case. In the end, all the evidence pointed to Laura taking her own life."

I stared down at our interlocked hands. That's why he'd offered to help me, why he'd pushed the chief of police to investigate Uncle Stan's case further. He'd stood where I was, desperately hoping it wasn't true. In a way, I gave him a chance at a do-over. If I hadn't been so deep in my own grief at the time, I might have seen the clues and put it together sooner, saving us both months of heartache.

But somehow, his grief, and the depth with which he'd loved his wife and the daughter they lost, only made me love him more.

I leaned forward to kiss him.

"I told you we should have stayed away a little longer," Elise's voice said from behind me.

I pulled back before my lips touched Mark's, and he groaned. I groaned inside along with him. For months I'd been daydreaming about what it would be like to kiss him, and now that I could, we kept getting interrupted. It was enough to make me want to scream.

"You have impeccable timing, Lise," Mark said.

Elise leaned against the wall at the foot of his bed and grinned. "I hope this means you two finally worked things out. I don't know if I could have stood you moping around much longer."

"I don't know." I tossed Mark a cheeky grin so he'd know I was teasing. "I'm not sure about the wisdom of dating a man who seems to have a death wish. Earlier this year he got himself shot at, and this time he drove into the backend of a semi truck."

Mark's forehead crinkled again. "What do you mean? I didn't drive into it. My brakes didn't work."

All the warmth in my body leeched out and pooled in my toes. Mark told me before that his truck was in the shop having the brakes fixed. They should have worked perfectly. Unless someone tampered with them.

# Chapter 18

Elise called Erik with the new information. I could tell by the way she crushed her lips together until they almost disappeared that his end of the conversation wasn't happening the way she'd expected. "He's going to send Quincey to take Mark's statement," she said after she disconnected, "but he thinks it's unlikely this had anything to do with Noah's case."

"It does seem like there isn't a connection," Grant said.

Elise and I glared at him in unison.

He held up his hands in surrender. "I'm only stating the facts as I see them."

Since Grant and Meagan had to get home to their kids, they took down a list of what Mark wanted them to bring back later and headed out. Elise and I decided to stay until Quincey arrived.

Mark still held onto my hand as though he never wanted to let go. While I couldn't speak for him, I knew I didn't. It felt unreal that something so good could come out of something as horrible as a car accident. "Do you want us to go, too, so you can rest?"

He shook his head. "Now that you're not working so hard to avoid me, I want in on this."

Elise dragged a chair from the other side of the room and updated him on our conversation with Stacey Rathmell.

"Tony might have had motive for Noah," Mark said, "but he'd have no reason to want to hurt me. I wouldn't even recognize his daughter."

I chewed the edge of my lip. Mark's accident did seem unconnected to Noah's attack and the explosion at the sugar shack. "It could be something you know. You examined Noah's wound, and you looked at the crime scene."

"All of that's in the records now."

I wanted to growl or stomp my foot. We were getting nowhere. Even in investigating Noah's attack, we still didn't have concrete evidence that Tony had done it. "Are there any common factors between all three events?"

"All the people who were injured are men," Mark said. "But I doubt this is a weird vendetta against the male gender."

I squeezed his hand. "Russ wasn't the only one injured. Another employee was burned by the sap, and she's a woman."

Elise punched one fist into the palm of her other hand. "And whoever sabotaged the reverse osmosis machine couldn't have known who'd be close by when it exploded."

This was the first I'd heard that they had clear results. "The lab is sure now that it was rigged?"

Elise nodded. "The pressure relief valve was soldered shut. They didn't set a timer or anything like that, but without a working valve, they had to know the machine would blow."

I couldn't sit still any more. I let go of Mark's hand with an apologetic smile. "I need to move. It helps me think." I paced the length of the short room, from window to door. "So two of the events were mechanical, but not the first, not Noah's accident."

"And two were at Sugarwood," Mark said. "My accident wasn't far from Quantum Mechanics."

I pivoted and headed back the other direction. It felt like there was no connection between the events, except that I knew all the people involved, which wasn't saying much given how small the town was. We had to be missing something.

Unless the connection was me. I stopped short.

Mark sat up straighter. "What is it?"

"I think we've been chasing the wrong goose." If I was wrong, I was going to sound like a narcissist, but that was a small risk in comparison. Because if I was right, everyone and everything I cared about could be in danger. "We might have sent Erik after the wrong person. I think I might be the link."

"You're not the link," Mark said, but his voice had the tone of someone who knew they were fighting against the truth and the truth scared them.

Elise had her professional demeanor back in place. "We have to figure this out before Quincey gets here. If someone were targeting you, how do they all connect?"

"Without Noah, we have no repairman and we're short-handed for the sugar season and for giving tours. Taking out our reverse osmosis machine on top of that came very close to sinking us. If we hadn't had a back-up and so many volunteers helping out, I would have had to drain my savings to get us through. And Mark's—"

My cheeks felt like I'd lain out in the sun too long. I almost said *Mark's the man I love.*

"I think everyone could see how I feel about Mark," I finished lamely.

I couldn't make myself look in his direction to see if he'd filled in the blanks anyway. I couldn't expect him to feel the same when we'd only officially begun dating a few minutes ago. Instead I focused my gaze on Elise.

"If someone wanted to hurt me, Mark, Sugarwood, and my dogs would be the best way to do it."

My dogs were the last ones unaffected, and they were vulnerable targets all alone in my house. Even though they were a Great Dane and a large Bullmastiff, someone could give them a poisoned piece of food and they'd eat it.

I held up a finger and scrambled to my purse. I yanked out my phone and dialed Russ' cell.

"How's Mark?" he asked before I could even say *hello.*

What was it with this town? It was like they had a system of signal flags set up that transferred news as soon as it happened. "He's going to be okay. We're waiting for Quincey to come talk to him, so I'll be a bit yet. Could you go to my house and take the dogs back home with you?"

I'd asked Russ to feed or walk them before, but never to take them home with him.

"Any particular reason?" His voice was too measured, like he knew he wasn't going to like what was coming. I'd dropped enough unpleasant ideas on him that he probably thought twice about even taking my calls anymore.

"I'm not sure yet, but I'm not comfortable with them being there alone." Or eating anything in my house. "Don't take their food. I'll buy a new bag on my way home."

Russ spoke again, but his voice was muffled, like he was talking to someone in the house with him with his hand over the phone.

"I'll head over now," he said. "Oliver's here with me talking over the possibility of filling in for Noah for repairs at least for the sugar season, so he says he'll walk there with me 'cause of my head."

My throat clogged. I might have to eventually tell Oliver that the attack on Noah had been my fault, however indirectly, just like his dismissal from the police station. After that, he might refuse to work for us anymore, and we'd be back to scratch for filling Noah's spot. "Thank him for me, okay?"

"Will do."

"Is there anything else you can think of?" Elise asked as soon as I disconnected.

"I don't think—" I dropped my face into my hands. There had been something else going wrong. I forced myself to look at them again. "Our sap lines are springing leaks that the manufacturer can't explain. They blamed it on squirrels, but Russ wasn't convinced."

Elise took her notebook and pen out. "Let's assume you're right. The real question is who'd want to hurt you."

I quirked a smile at her. "You didn't like me much when we first met."

She pulled a face. "Hardy har har."

I sat back beside Mark and took his hand again. It felt so good to be able to do that. Besides, I'd need the moral support if I was going to try to figure out how many people might hate me enough to sabotage my business and seriously injure the people close to me. "My ex-boyfriend would love to see me dead, but he's already in prison."

Mark cocked an eyebrow. "I'm not the only one who didn't share everything."

"She can give you the full story later," Elise said. "Right now, we need a list of names, and unless her ex hired a hitman, who he is and what he did isn't important at the moment."

Most of the people with a violent level of fury at me were in jail. That was the problem.

"Ashley at Tom McClanahan's office hates me for some unknown reason, but I don't think she'd resort to this level of crazy or that she'd have the mechanical skills to do it."

"She hates you because of Mark. She might have cut your brakes, but not his," Elise said matter-of-factly. "She's wanted Mark ever since Laura died."

Aside from what Ashley might have deduced about Mark's feelings, the rumors around town said I'd been playing him, along with Erik, Dave, and Noah. She could have just waited it out.

Holy crap. The rumors. "What if Stacey heard the rumors and believed that Noah was cheating on her with me?"

Elise gave the slow I'm-thinking-it-through nod. "She's waited all these years for him, her eighteenth birthday comes, they consummate their relationship, and then she hears that Noah's been linked to you...that could have pushed her over the edge, especially since she'd have been embarrassed that everyone was right about Noah only wanting one thing from her. It would have seemed like he did only want one thing, he just didn't want to risk going to jail for it."

Mark raised his hand like a child waiting his turn in school. Elise and I had kind of been dominating the conversation. "Unless Stacey's a particularly tall woman, the angle of the wound is wrong."

Elise swiveled toward me. "Noah could have been down on his knees or bent over, examining something on your horse's leg."

He only would have been doing one of those things outside the stall, with Key in cross-ties. But it was possible, and it would have been easier for someone to sneak up on him if that was the case. "I did see flecks on Key's front leg that could have been blood spatter. Do you think Stacey's strong enough to haul an unconscious man's body five to ten feet?"

"She looked it," Elise said. "She'd need to be able to lift heavy parts and equipment."

I didn't want it to be Tony, but I didn't want it to be Stacey, either. "Do we have any other reasonable options?"

"Not unless you think Georgiana Abbott was lying to you."

She hadn't been lying to me, but in my shock over how much Noah owed, I hadn't remembered to ask an important question. "I didn't ask if she had ideas about who else might hold a grudge against Noah."

I pulled the card Georgiana gave me from my purse. True to form, the embossed letters only said *G. Abbott.*

Her bartender—Devin I think she called him—answered. "She's out. Want to leave a message?"

The impression I'd gotten when I was there, based on Devin's reaction to me and on what he said to Georgiana about me when he brought me to her office, was that he was more than simply the bartender. "Maybe you can answer my question instead. Did Georgiana tell you why I came to see her?"

"Yup."

Close-mouthed and loyal. It was the worst combination when trying to get information from someone. I'd have to make it clear that I wasn't after Georgiana. "I know Georgiana wasn't involved in what happened to Noah, but I wanted to know if he had problems with anyone else there that you two knew about."

I almost said *maybe another regular*, but that might have shut down any hope I had of Devin talking. Georgiana's establishment seemed like it valued its regulars. And their privacy. She'd only talked to me about Noah because of what had happened to him.

"He had a screaming match with some jailbait out in the parking lot recently. Not that unusual around here, though. Seems like every week there's some family member upset about the tabs our clients run up. We stay out of it."

*Jailbait* usually referred to an underage girl. Despite her true age, Stacey didn't look over eighteen, so it could have been her. Which was the opposite of what I'd hoped to hear. "Do you remember what she looked like?"

"Can't say as I do. If you want more than what I've told you, you can try Georgiana later."

I thanked him and ended the call, but I'd blown it. The way I'd phrased the question had given him an easy out.

Elise and Mark were watching me, their eyebrows raised in an eerie mirror image. Though, admittedly, Mark's eyebrows seemed a little less mobile at present due to the bruises on his face.

I shoved my phone back into my purse. "Noah had an argument with a teenage girl outside of the Bar & Grill recently."

Even as I said it, something about our theory felt like it didn't fit, like a piece taken from one puzzle trying to be forced into another.

Elise pushed an escaping bobby pin back into her bun. "I think I'm going to go to the station and talk to Erik personally. If he's worried about the brass, we can always run this by a district attorney and see if they think there's enough to make a case with it all connected."

Mark yawned, then winced. His battered face didn't make him any less attractive to me, but for his sake, I hoped it healed soon.

I skimmed my fingertips along his jawline. "Now you *are* tired."

"A little." He started to yawn again, but his mouth barely opened before he clamped it down. "You two don't have to wait for Quincey. I might be able to catch a nap before he comes."

I rose to my feet, and my gaze skipped to his lips. I wanted to kiss him goodbye, but I didn't want our first kiss to be in front of Elise. I pressed a kiss into his forehead instead. "Call me when they're ready to release you, okay?"

He nodded. His eyes had drifted to half-mast.

Elise and I left. Quincey came out of the elevator as we went in.

We rode down in silence since we were the only ones to get on. A niggling sensation, like I was missing something important, crept into my mind. I tried to ignore it and blame the tension on the elevator, but it wouldn't budge.

We left the elevator, and the automatic doors at the emergency room entrance swished open for us. We stepped out into the dark. The snow had returned to flurries that were only visible in the street light halos.

Elise spun her keys around on her finger. "This is definitely not the way I thought today would end."

I stopped walking. Keys! That's what felt wrong. "We lock the sugar shack when no one's working."

Elise turned around and her nose crinkled. "Okay?" She drew the word out in that *I don't know where you're going with this* type of way.

"We've had a couple of days where the sap wasn't running and so we weren't working in the sugar shack where the reverse osmosis machine was. That's the only time someone could have sabotaged it. Otherwise our employees would have noticed someone tampering with it."

"Okay," Elise said in the same drawn-out tone.

I pointed at her keys. "You need a set of keys to get in. The only set that the saboteur could have gotten access to were Noah's. We didn't think to take them at first, and they were sitting with his clothes in the cubby hole until I took them back the other day."

Elise held her hands out to the side and shrugged her shoulders. "I'm not following."

I was kind of taking the circuitous route to saying what I wanted to say, but I didn't want to jump to conclusions, and working through it verbally helped me make sure it all hung together.

"Stacey told us they wouldn't let her in to see Noah. You promised to have her put on the list, remember? That means she couldn't have taken the keys, and her defense council will be sure to point that out. But I did see Tony at the hospital the other night when I came to pick up Russ, and when I went up to Noah's room to check in on him, no one was around to watch who was coming and going. Tony could have been bringing the keys back after using them to get in to the sugar shack or taking them to make a copy."

"Okay." The same word, but this time with the sense that she was finally following my rabbit trails. "But if we think this was about you from the beginning, and not Noah, then we're back to our original problem. Tony has no reason to want to hurt you or Mark."

I headed for the police cruiser again. This case didn't make sense. Every theory had a hole in it. Tony didn't have a reason to hurt me, and I'd always gotten the impression that he liked me...or at least that he found my propensity to wreck my car amusing. His only motivation in all of this was protecting his daughter.

But maybe that was the answer. "What if they were in on it together?"

# Chapter 19

Elise's eyebrows formed pointy triangles. She unlocked the car. We climbed in, and she cranked the heat but stayed parked. "Even if they were in it together, that still doesn't explain why Tony would go along with hurting you. It's so out of character."

It didn't, and it was. I pressed my hands closer to a vent. Maybe if I warmed up, my brain would work better. Right now it wanted to jump back and forth between *Mark's not married* and how cold I was. I needed to think like my dad. If his client was accused of this crime, how would he spin the Tony–Stacey element to cast more than reasonable doubt?

"We're thinking that Tony's motive was protecting his daughter, and Stacey's motive was jealousy because she believed the rumors. So let's assume Stacey and Noah fought about the rumors and Stacey hit him with his own wrench. She goes running to her dad, and he sabotages the reverse osmosis machine to make it less obvious why Noah was attacked?"

Elise finally put the car into drive. She drummed four fingers along the steering wheel. "What about your sap lines, though? Didn't you say you found leaks before Noah's attack?"

We had. The sap lines had leaks when we turned the machines on in the morning, and I'd seen Noah walking and talking then. "I wonder if Noah could have caught Stacey or figured out that she was sabotaging the lines and that's part of what they argued over."

"Maybe." Elise's lips narrowed. "But that still doesn't explain Mark."

It didn't. He hadn't known anything that could prove Stacey did this. Maybe if it'd been my car I could understand it. Tony knew I had a picture of Stacey with Noah, and that I was asking around. That might have made him nervous enough that he felt he needed to stop me.

Oh no. I grabbed the arm rest. "The last time I was in at Quantum Mechanics, Tony thought I was there to pick up Mark's truck for him. He might have compromised the brakes, expecting I'd be the one driving it when they went."

After Elise dropped me and two fresh bags of dog food off, I grabbed the dogs from Russ and a pair of boots and latex kitchen gloves and went back to the stables. Now that I knew we were probably looking for a wrench, I wanted to make one more pass of the crime scene.

I flicked on the lights in the stable and squeezed my hands into the gloves. Even though fingerprints on anything I might find couldn't be used in court, that didn't mean the police couldn't use them at all. The main things I wanted to figure out were whether we'd guessed the right weapon and whether whoever did this brought it with them or used what was at hand. If they'd brought a weapon with them, that meant premeditation.

I went through the tack room again while Toby and Velma enjoyed themselves sniffing the hay bales and around the stalls. Noah's neat labels specified where every piece of equipment went. Nothing seemed to be missing or out of place. I shined a flashlight over it all for extra visibility and moved the pieces around, looking behind them. Nothing.

We'd already looked through the horse stalls, so I skipped those and the bin where we kept the brushes and other small items. None of them were hard enough or the right shape to create Noah's wound, and I'd been all through the container in the following days while caring for the horses.

The only place left to search was Noah's toolbox. It still sat where I'd seen it the day I found his body.

I opened the lid. Inside, Noah had taped an inventory to the lid with neat lines of silver duct tape.

I hung my head back and stared at the ceiling for a moment. None of the tools inside looked splattered with blood, so the only way to know if something was missing was to take it all out and compare it to Noah's inventory list.

My eyes already felt gritty from the long day, but it didn't seem like the attacker planned to stop. Figuring out exactly what the police needed to search for brought us one step closer to stopping Tony, Stacey, or whoever might be behind it all.

I laid the tools out, using my phone to search images and descriptions of anything I didn't recognize by name. As embarrassing as it was, that turned out to be seventy-five percent of the items. My family were apartment dwellers. Whenever anything broke, we called the super.

An hour later, only one item was missing—Noah's largest open-ended wrench. Noah was too meticulous to misplace his tools. If the wrench wasn't there, I'd bet my farm—literally—that whoever attacked him took it.

I typed the type of wrench into my search bar. The images that came up showed a horseshoe-shaped end. I texted Elise with the brand and style of wrench.

I'd found the assailant's weapon, and it was missing.

"Erik got the warrant for Quantum Mechanics to look for the wrench," Elise said when she called me two days later. "The fact that Mark's brakes were sabotaged while there and he's a county employee who was helping investigate Noah's attacker convinced the judge that there was justifiable cause to search."

I stripped off the sterile gloves I'd put on a few hours ago when Nancy had started teaching me the process of making maple butter (which, as it turns out, has absolutely no butter in it at all). The process was delicate, but Nancy promised to teach me all the tricks she'd learned in her ten years of working at Sugarwood and cooking at Short Stack during the non-sugar season.

Since we were between batches, I tossed the gloves and let Nancy know I needed to take the phone call.

"Have they executed the warrant yet?" I asked Elise.

"Yesterday morning. Erik took all the wrenches for comparison and analysis."

She paused. It had to be for emphasis. I took the few seconds to step outside the back door where I'd have a bit more quiet and privacy.

"They found it," Elise said. "They found a wrench with trace elements of blood that matched the description of Noah's tools you gave us."

A bevy of questions poured into my mind, like *Were they able to get a big enough sample to compare the blood to Noah's?* But one question outweighed the others in importance. "Whose tools was it with?"

"Stacey's. Erik brought both Stacey and Tony in for questioning this morning."

I walked away from the building and back. My mom used to always say that only lies were neat and tidy. The truth was usually messy. That Stacey had held on to the wrench and kept it at Quantum Mechanics felt like it belonged more in the neat-and-tidy category, but maybe sometimes things could be simple. My mom wasn't always right.

"What did they say when Erik interrogated them?"

"Stacey claimed she'd never seen the wrench before, that it didn't belong to her, that she didn't know how it got in with her tools."

All things I would have expected her to say. Elise seemed to have the same talent as Mark with impressions because, even though I doubted she intended it, I could hear the teenage angst in her recitation of Stacey's reaction. "And Tony?"

"He had nothing to do with Noah's attack, he said. Even though we couldn't prove it, Erik took a gamble and asked why he went to the hospital to see Noah given their history. Tony claimed it was to 'make peace' with him. He denied knowing anything about the keys."

The skepticism in Elise's voice matched what I felt. People didn't tend to change without some catalyst. Granted, Noah's coma could have been the catalyst, but Tony's reaction when he saw the picture I showed to Oliver didn't seem like that of a man who'd let bygones be bygones.

I moved into a patch of sunlight in the hope of warming up so I didn't have to take this conversation inside. Eventually everyone in Fair Haven would learn what had happened, but I wasn't going to be the one to hasten it by speaking around my employees. "The DA might still be willing to charge Stacey based on the weapon and a motive even if Erik couldn't get anything more solid from them."

"He won't have to." Elise's pride radiated through the phone. "He got Tony to confess."

Based on her tone of voice, she'd been holding that back for effect. "You could have led with that."

"I could have, but I thought you'd want the whole story." Now there was a smile in her voice. It faded away as soon as she spoke again. "We decided to lay out for each of them the case against the other. Stacey held strong to her story and insisted her dad never would have hurt Noah, either. Tony confessed to attacking Noah and said Stacey didn't know anything about it."

I pushed a hand against the building wall. That sounded a lot more like what a man trying to protect his daughter would do than what a man who was actually guilty would do.

A bad taste coated my tongue, like spoiled milk, and unease settled in my chest. I'd initiated this conspiracy theory, and I'd pointed the finger in Tony and Stacey's direction, but something still didn't feel right. "Why hang on to the wrench, then? Why not toss it into the lake?"

"Maybe he didn't realize it could be tested for blood later."

Not likely. With all the crime shows on TV anymore, you'd have to be a recluse to not realize you basically had to drop a weapon in bleach if you wanted to rid it of all traces.

"I realize you didn't want it to be Tony or Stacey," Elise said, "but at least you and Mark and Noah should all be safe now."

Assuming we had the right people. Maybe it was the investigator's version of buyer's remorse, but the wrench bothered me. "Do you think it's possible someone planted the wrench?"

"Possible, yes. But I don't think that's what happened." Elise had switched to her soft, mothering voice again. "Tony confessed. He wouldn't have done that if he wasn't guilty or convinced Stacey was guilty or if he was protecting her because they worked it out together."

A cloud moved over the sun, a gust of wind bit into my cheeks, and I shivered. Tony and Stacey weren't experienced criminals. It was possible that whoever really did it panicked when they realized what they'd done and they'd taken the wrench with them because their fingerprints were on it, then didn't know what to do with it. A lot more possible than there being a different attacker who'd thought this through carefully and methodically enough to keep the weapon and plant it.

Except they'd found the wrench in *Stacey's* toolbox. "Tony had to be involved, otherwise they couldn't have gotten the keys to the sugar shack. But if he did it alone or he was involved, why wouldn't he have put the wrench in his toolbox? No father who'd go to prison for his child would knowingly leave condemning evidence someplace that would point to that child as the guilty party. You're a mom. Does that sound like something you'd do?"

Elise said something I couldn't hear, but the tone sounded like an invective. "Let's say you convinced me that it might not be Tony or Stacey. His confession makes it almost impossible that we'll convince anyone else."

"Were there fingerprints on the wrench?"

"None. Not even Noah's."

The uncomfortable feeling in the pit of my stomach grew. No one wiped down a weapon, then put it with their own belongings. "What if we looked for an alibi for him? We could break his confession that way. He should have been working at Quantum Mechanics at that time of day. Someone must have seen him."

A creak sounded in the background on Elise's end, a sound I recognized as the much-needing-oil door to the ladies' restroom at the police station. Given that she was the only female officer, it was one place she could be guaranteed privacy unless a civilian came in.

"This town...the people here..." Elise said. "They're loyal to their own. We can try, but if the guys at Quantum Mechanics learn Tony confessed, they're not going to alibi him out, regardless of the truth. They'll let him take the fall for this and save Stacey if that's what he wants to do."

There had to be a hole in Tony's story that we could shove a knife through and tear it open. Otherwise, whoever really did this was going to get away with it, and an innocent man would go to prison. "Did he confess to everything, or only to attacking Noah? Maybe you could convince him to take back his confession if you can show that you know he's lying."

"I don't think that'll work, but let me go check his written confession."

We disconnected, and Nancy and I had almost finished another batch of maple butter when my phone vibrated in my pocket, letting me know a text had come in. The time between when it arrived and when we were done so I could answer felt three times as long as it actually was.

*He admitted to attacking Noah and sabotaging your RO machine and Mark's brakes,* Elise wrote. *No mention of your sap lines.*

Everything he'd included, he could have learned about through the Fair Haven gossip chain, but not the sap lines. Only the real attacker would have known about those.

*Did he say why he did it?* I texted back.

Elise's reply came fast, like she'd been waiting for a response from me. *Gave a reason for Noah but refused for the rest of it.*

Those two together meant that, at best, Tony was covering for Stacey, and at worst, we still had no idea who the real attacker was.

And no way to prove either.

# Chapter 20

"Would it be unchivalrous of me to ask you out on our first official date and then ask you to drive?" Mark said when he called me the next day.

This relationship was already far different from the one I'd had with Peter. He'd always wanted to stay in. At the time, I'd thought it'd been a sign of how much he loved and desired me, but the truth turned out to be the exact opposite. He hadn't wanted anyone to see us out together. He also hadn't spent hours talking to me on the phone when we couldn't be together the way Mark did. It was too bad I couldn't have seen the flaws and red flags in that relationship when I was in it rather than only in hindsight. Everything might have turned out very different if I had.

But, then again, maybe if I had, I never would have ended up in Fair Haven, and while my life wasn't perfect here, I was happier than I'd ever been in DC.

I smiled into the phone even though he couldn't see it. "Since you have a broken wrist and a totaled truck, I can give you a pass this time."

Though technically I'd have to borrow Russ' truck to do that. With all that'd been happening with Tony, Quantum Mechanics had a backlog on repairs.

"We could go to A Salt & Battery for your favorite fish and chips dinner," Mark said.

My mouth watered. The fish and chips at A Salt & Battery rivaled any DC restaurant in my opinion, but the last time we'd been to A Salt & Battery together, I'd learned the meaning of *if looks could kill*.

"Unless you'd rather wait until I'm back to pink in color and less like a Benzite."

I laughed so hard a little snort slipped out. The fact that Mark could reference the blue- and green-skinned race from *Star Trek* in normal conversation only made him that much more attractive to me. "I wouldn't mind being seen with you in public even if you were bald like a Benzite, but the waitress at A Salt & Battery seems to hate me, probably because she's heard the same rumors as Elise."

"Then we'll have to be so enamored with each other that she'll know the rumors aren't true."

I couldn't come up with a good argument for that, especially given the warmth it sent through my body.

I wished that I had when we entered A Salt & Battery and we had to pass Stacey Rathmell to reach an open table. Her face had a puffy look to it, and she sat hunched over her coffee cup, her arms encircling it almost like she was protecting it from the rest of the world.

That she was able to hold herself together at all spoke to an inner strength. She'd lost her fiancé and her father in the span of a month. Not only that, but everyone would believe her father was the one who'd taken her fiancé from her.

Stacey looked up as we passed and met my gaze. Her eyes were red-rimmed and hollow and very, very angry.

We should have gotten take-out.

We weaved our way to the back of the restaurant where the booths were. I'd always liked a booth better than a table. Mandy from The Sunburnt Arms and her niece (I recognized her from the photos Mandy had proudly shown me during my stay) waved at us as we passed. Coming from a big city, I still fought to find the balance between loving the fact that I was recognized and known and feeling like I was living in a Fair Haven-sized fish bowl. Right now it was a bit of both. It would have been nice to go out with Mark without being recognized by everyone, and seeing Stacey brought my mind back to something I'd been considering if we couldn't break Tony's confession or find the real attacker in time.

Mark stepped aside and let me pick which side of the booth I wanted. I expected him to sit on the other side of the table, but he slid in next to me.

"I'll be your shield against grumpy waitresses," he said.

He did look a bit like a fierce warrior with his bruised face. The edges of his bruises were more a yellow-green now than a purple-blue. If only he could be a human shield between me and the growing list of people who seemed to want to harm me. With Tony in custody, the police weren't looking for Noah's attacker anymore, so whoever had really done it was still roaming around free and without the fear of scrutiny.

I leaned over and kissed him on the cheek, very gently.

His mouth quirked up at one corner like he was still afraid a full smile would hurt. "What was that for?"

"Wanting to be my hero." I picked at the tablecloth. I should probably keep the conversation light, but now that I had Mark back, I coveted his advice. He'd already heard about the Tony–Stacey interrogation through Elise, so I didn't need to fill him in. "I was thinking about offering to represent Tony as his defense council."

"Does that mean you think he's innocent or that you think he's—"

A shadow fell over our table. I looked up, expecting the waitress, but instead Oliver's wide eyes peered back at me. All of Fair Haven seemed to be in A Salt & Battery tonight.

"I won't interrupt you long." He shoved his hands in his pockets. "Since I saw you here, I thought you both might want to know they're taking Noah off life support tomorrow. You know, in case you wanted to go say goodbye."

My tongue seemed to melt into the bottom of my mouth. There was only one reason they'd be removing him from life support when he hadn't shown any improvement. He was brain dead. *I'm sorry* seemed insufficient.

"Thank you," I said instead.

The waitress came and swapped places with Oliver. I texted Russ and Elise with the news about Noah in case they wanted to stop by the hospital to see him one last time. Elise hadn't seemed close with Noah, but I didn't want to take the chance and violate our newly formed friendship by assuming.

When the waitress delivered our food, she glared at me a little less than usual. It might have been the way we were openly holding hands on top of the table, or it might have been the fact that I was here, with Mark, when he looked his worst. Either way, the ice daggers she usually shot at me from her eyes had blunted edges by the time Mark paid the bill.

Mandy and her niece were gone, but Oliver still sat at one of the tables, and so did Stacey. I nodded to Oliver and tucked in closer to Mark.

He could have easily ended up like Noah thanks to the crash. I could very well be the one sitting at a table alone tonight, wondering how I'd move on from it. Wondering if there was any way to move beyond so big a loss.

Had someone told Stacey about Noah being removed from life support? More than me or Russ or anyone else, she deserved to know what was about to happen tomorrow and to go by the hospital if she wanted to. That's something I would have wanted if I were in her place.

When we came alongside her table, I stopped, pulling Mark to a halt with me.

Stacey's gaze jumped from our intertwined hands up to my face. The malice shown by the waitress before seemed like a kindergarten spat compared to the way Stacey looked at me now.

"Don't," she said, the word coming out in a hiss. "Whatever you've come to say to ease your conscience, I don't want to hear it."

Had Mark not been at my side, preventing me from stepping back, I might have retreated.

He caught my gaze and then tilted his head toward Stacey in a silent *You want me to handle this?*

I gave my head a tiny shake. I'd happily let Mark protect me from waitresses and intruders, but this bat-

tle was mine. Stacey's problem was with me, presumably because she'd figured out how I'd been involved in
the search of Quantum Mechanics. Mark defending me
wouldn't resolve her issues toward me. "I wanted to be
sure you'd heard. They're removing Noah from life
support tomorrow. If you'd like to see him again, you'll
want to go tonight."

I'd have to text Erik as soon as we left to ensure
Stacey had been placed on the list. It'd feel like a cruel
trick if I told her to go and they wouldn't let her in.

She sucked her bottom lip in and her skin-toned
took on a yellow tinge, like the beginning of jaundice.
She swiped a hand across her stomach, then stood and
planted her fists on the table top. "So many people
were better off before you came to this town. Do you
have any idea how many lives you've ruined? Why
couldn't you have stayed wherever you came from?"

My stomach felt like it caved in from a hard blow. I
hadn't expected gratitude, but I also hadn't expected a
direct attack. Whether it was her upbringing or her
natural reserve, at least she kept her voice down. The
only ones close enough to hear us were Oliver and our
waitress. It spared a little bit of my pride at least.

Stacey dropped a $5 bill on the table and strode out
before I could come up with an appropriate reply.

All I could think to do in response was something
practical. I called Elise and left a message when I didn't
get her, asking her to check that Stacey was on the list

of people allowed to visit Noah. I sent Erik a text of the same just in case.

Then I stood by the window, staring at my phone.

Mark slid an arm around my waist and shepherded me out the door. The snap of the wind outside and the warmth of his touch brought me back into focus, but I still had no idea how to respond to Stacey's attack.

Because her accusations felt right. I'd tried to do good and to help people, but the lines weren't always clear.

We climbed into Russ' truck, and Mark laid a hand on my arm. "I know you're going to have a hard time believing this right now, but you've made a lot of lives better, too."

By the time I got home after visiting Noah for the final time, I'd almost convinced myself that Mark was right and Stacey was wrong.

Right up until I found the blue box of chocolate-covered raisins on my porch with a note: *A treat for your dogs.*

Erik stood next to me on my steps, staring down at the blue box of candy with the graphic of a smiling chocolate-covered raisin. Leaving a chocolate bar would have been threat enough, but to leave something with both chocolate and raisins sent a clear message.

They knew what could hurt my dogs, and it wasn't an *if* but a *when* that they'd do it.

"You didn't need to come yourself," I said. "I know you're busy. Quincey or Elise could have handled it."

Erik pulled out an evidence bag. "It's not my call anymore. They've hired the new chief, and I was sent on this call as a regular officer."

He'd been making decisions about calling in warrants and interrogating suspects only a day or two ago. The change in leadership must be fresh. "Should I offer congratulations or condolences?"

"Maybe a little of both." He stooped and slid the chocolate box into the bag. "I'll see if we can get any prints, but given how careful this guy's been so far, it's not likely."

I should simply let him go, but a noose of fear choked me.

*You're being a baby*, the accusing voice in my head said. But I couldn't shake it. "Could you take a quick look through the house? Just to be sure."

He nodded. "I was going to suggest it."

He dropped the evidence bag in his car while I unlocked the door. I let him go in alone. The dogs' barking signaled when he reached the laundry room.

He was back out in five minutes. "It's all clear. I even checked the closets."

I thanked him for coming out anyway and didn't offer him a cup of coffee the way I would have before. The new chief might not look kindly on him lingering, and I didn't want to risk being the cause of him receiving a reprimand on the first day.

Even with Erik's assurance that the house was free of intruders, I couldn't settle down enough to sleep in my own bed. By 11:00, I gave up and dragged my comforter downstairs to the couch. I let the dogs out on my way. If there was a night when I wanted them both where I could see them, it was tonight.

I'd just drifted off when my phone rang. I fished around between my couch cushions and managed to grab it on the final ring.

"Sorry to wake you," Erik said. His voice sounded a bit distant, like he was on Bluetooth. He must be driving home from work.

I didn't see the point in denying that he'd woken me up, but it must be late if he were apologizing. I scrubbed at my bleary eyes. Both dogs still laid on their beds next to the couch. Velma had her head resting on Toby's back leg. "Is something wrong?"

Erik cleared his throat, which was an indicator that I wasn't going to like what he had to say next. "I'm still trying to work a way around it, but the new chief thought fingerprinting the candy box would be a waste of time and departmental resources. He said we don't have enough proof that this was malicious or connected to any of the other crimes. It could have been someone trying to be nice who didn't realize that chocolate and raisins are poisonous for dogs."

Right, and I was going to wake up in the morning a five-foot-eight model who could walk in stilettos without breaking an ankle. But it wasn't Erik's fault, so I couldn't take my frustration out on him. "Has he been updated on everything that's been happening?"

"Yeah. Updated and in favor of closing the case. He's not interested in questioning Tony's confession."

Double great. If the saboteur kept going as it looked like he or she planned to, it'd eventually become clear that Tony was innocent, but by then someone else might be dead.

"And Nicole?" Erik said. "You need to stay clear of the police station for a while. The new chief was sent here to make sure no one bends even part of a rule."

# Chapter 21

My doorbell rang the next morning as I was getting ready to walk to the sugar shack, and the dogs leaped up from their spots on the floor, the hair on the backs of their necks up, their barking nearly deafening. Even though Velma was a girl and still growing, her bark was already nearly as deep as Toby's.

I headed for the door, the muscles in my back clenched so tightly that it felt like painful spasms sending tendrils out under my skin. Normally I would have put the dogs into the laundry room when someone came to the door, but I'd felt exposed ever since finding out the new chief of police wasn't looking for whoever left the chocolate-covered raisins on my steps. Neither of my dogs had an aggressive bone in their bodies, but I was pretty sure they'd find a protective one if someone tried to hurt me.

I checked the peephole and got an eyeful of Oliver's owl-like gaze. The tension in my back released, and I opened the door.

The dogs tried to push past me. I stuffed my feet into my shoes and stepped outside, closing the door on them. "Sorry about the noise. They don't know how to tell friends from intruders yet."

Oliver took off his glasses and cleaned one lens on the corner of his shirt. His rapid blinks were faster than usual. He put his glasses back on a little crooked. "Noah's gone."

Before I could process what he'd said, he pulled me into a tight hug, squishing my nose up against his bony chest. A headache bloomed above my eyes, the scent of gasoline overwhelming my senses.

"The doctor called me a few minutes ago, and I didn't have anywhere else to go," he said, his breath poofing the top of my hair.

Tears pressed against my eyes, and I blinked them back. Noah was gone. Last night, when I couldn't sleep, I'd almost convinced myself that Noah would be one of those miracle cases—the ones where the doctors take them off life support and they start breathing on their own.

But he wasn't.

Oliver squeezed me tighter. My gut instinct said *pull away*—his hug made me uncomfortable in a way I couldn't quantify—but Oliver hadn't had anyone to come to in his grief but me. I only knew pieces about their childhood and abusive family, but no one should be alone in their time of grief. I understood loneliness. It wasn't just the lack of support that made it so hard. It was the feeling like no one would miss you if you vanished, and the feeling like there must be something wrong with you to make you so isolated. Having to grieve alone only made those emotions more intense.

I wriggled my arms free and patted Oliver awkwardly on the back. A car drove by on the laneway, heading in the direction of the sugar shack and setting my dogs barking again, buying me a little time to figure out what to say.

Even then, the only thing I could come up with was, "I'm so sorry."

I gave the backward lean that should have signaled to him the hug was done. He didn't let go right away. In fact it was a full five count before he released me.

I stepped back and untwisted my torqued sweater. Then took another step in case he tried to hug me again. It was probably awful of me, but I didn't want to be held by him.

"Would you come with me?" he asked. "To see him. I don't want to go alone."

Shouldn't there have been someone else? I'd only talked to him a few times. Oliver had to have work friends or something. Maybe he didn't realize how many people would be there for him if he needed them—I hadn't—but surely he had more people who'd rally around him now.

He took off his glasses and polished that same lens again. "I thought, since he worked for you, you might like to see him too. For closure, you know."

The rumors had clearly made me paranoid, and I was imagining things in others' thoughtfulness. I'd be a jerk to say *no*. "Sure. Let me put the dogs away and grab my purse and coat."

I ducked in, settled the dogs in their crates, and sent a quick text to Mark and Russ to call me when they could. I didn't want to give them the news about Noah via text.

I joined Oliver back outside and locked my door.

We headed down the walkway, and he grabbed my hand.

Okay, so I hadn't imagined that he was getting a little too personal before.

I yanked my hand free. Had the rumors about me given him the wrong idea about me, about me and No-ah, or about my availability? He'd seen me with Mark yesterday. Surely he wasn't sleazy enough to use his cousin's death to come on to me. I wasn't that pretty or that great.

"Look, Oliver—"

"Sorry about that." He shook his head in a *let's drop it* way and opened the passenger-side door of his truck for me. Unlike Mark's truck, Oliver's only had a single bench seat, no back seat.

"I'm a little unsteady," he said.

I climbed in and he closed the door for me. I'd let it drop. Grief could make people do silly things. After Noah's funeral, though, I needed to make a point to avoid Oliver. Mark meant too much to me to jeopardize our relationship by being around a man who couldn't keep his hands to himself. When Mark responded to my text, to be on the safe side, I'd even tell him about what Oliver had done.

Oliver took the turn out of Sugarwood's driveway a little fast, and I grabbed onto the door handle to steady myself. If I'd known he was that kind of a driver, I would have suggested I follow him in Russ' truck. Fast turns wouldn't have made me edgy on clear, dry roads, but we'd had another snow last night, and the roads could still be slick. Just because Oliver grew up with snow didn't mean he knew how to drive safely in it, and I really didn't want to end up in a ditch with him. That would definitely set people talking.

An aqua-colored car pulled out of the Sugarwood driveway not long after us. It was the only one I'd seen all day. Our tour bookings were half of what Russ had on record from last year.

Who could I have hurt badly enough that they'd do this to all of us? To Noah?

Oliver hit the brakes a bit late for the red light and an empty soda bottle and a hand-sized rectangular box slid out from under the seat. I nudged the soda bottle back and touched my heel to the box to do the same.

The blue color and the size—close to the length and width of my palm—made me stop. It looked a lot like the chocolate-covered raisin box left on my porch. But that was silly.

A zing hit me in the chest. Unless it wasn't silly.

Oliver smelled like gasoline, even when he wasn't wearing his work clothes, and I'd gotten a fume headache when I stepped into the barn the day I found Noah. Oliver had a reason to hate me. He had the technical knowledge to sabotage the reverse osmosis machine and Mark's truck, and he'd had access to Noah's keys. And he'd been with Russ when I asked him to take my dogs because I was afraid of someone poisoning them.

I tried to make it look like I was kicking the discarded box back under the seat as well while trying to shift it for a better look at the box to see if it had the smiling chocolate-covered raisin. If it was the same box, I could jump out of this truck and run before the light turned green. If I was wrong about Oliver, the worst that would happen is I'd look crazy. Most people in town thought I was a heartbreaking floosy anyway, so crazy seemed like a step up.

I squished the box too hard between my heel and the arch of my other foot. It popped up onto its side, flashing the smiling chocolate-covered raisin image at me.

And drawing Oliver's gaze.

My gaze met Oliver's, and the expression on his face, like a falcon that'd spotted its prey, told me more than the box did. It'd been him all along.

# Chapter 22

I hit the button on my seat belt with one hand and reached for the door handle with the other. My seatbelt released, but the door stayed closed. I yanked again.

"Doors automatically lock when the truck's in drive," Oliver said, his voice overly calm, as if I hadn't just tried to leap from his vehicle.

Some trucks had those tiny sliding windows in the back windshield. I glanced back, and my chest caved in. His rear window was solid.

The aqua car from Sugarwood pulled to a stop behind us. I could try to signal the driver for help, but they'd probably only think I was waving at them.

I turned back to the front. The light turned green, and Oliver hit the gas, pushing me back against the seat. I snapped my seatbelt into place. As little as I wanted to be here with him, I wanted to be thrown through his windshield even less.

"This was only supposed to be about getting pictures I could send to Mark, showing you cheating on him," Oliver said. "I already sent him an anonymous text telling him you were. But now that you've figured it out, I'm going to have to get rid of you and the drunk I hired to take the photos."

My head spun and my stomach went queasy like I was carsick even though I'd never struggled with motion sickness before. Being in a car with someone who wanted to hurt you was one of the worst possible scenarios because you were trapped. I had to keep a clear head. I had to find a way out. Otherwise, not only would I be dead, but Mark would think another woman had abandoned him.

My mouth was dry enough that I had to lick my lips before I could get any words out. "You've planned all this carefully up until now. That means you're smart enough to realize that spur-of-the-moment murders are sloppy murders. You'll get caught."

Oliver's slow blink-blink sent a shiver over my arms.

"I am smart. Smarter than you. All I need to do is disappear as well and send Mark a text from your phone telling him you're running away with me. I can easily start over anywhere, and with the reputation you have in Fair Haven, no one will think you didn't take off with me."

I pressed a hand over my mouth and swallowed down bile. Would Mark believe it? It wouldn't matter to me either way—I'd be dead—but it'd destroy him if he did. As if not dying wasn't a strong enough motivator, that thought alone gave me an extra reason to need to escape.

Except all Oliver needed to do was keep the doors locked, and he'd be able to overpower me when we stopped. In a space where I could move, I knew enough about self-defense that I might be able to fight him off and run. In the truck, he could use his superior size and strength to pin me and crush my windpipe, and I wasn't going to be able to stop him.

I could try one more tactic to talk him out of this, but it seemed like a vain hope. "Why would you want to hurt Mark that way? I thought you liked him. And Russ."

"This isn't about hurting them." Oliver squinched his nose up. "It was about hurting you and taking away the things you care about the same way you took away the things I cared about. My job at the police station. The one relative I had who was worth something. You're the one who had to be nosy about that box and wreck everything."

As if I'd asked to be taken out into the woods and murdered. Talking to him was *not* going to work, but I wanted to know one thing in case I didn't make it out of this. "If it was all about hurting me, then why kill your own cousin?"

"Shut up." Oliver's voice was so cold that it sent an image of him torturing me before killing me spiraling through my head. "Noah betrayed me. I asked him to help me sabotage Sugarwood so you'd lose the farm, and he refused. He said he'd go to the police if I did anything. I'd already cut your sap lines, so he didn't leave me a choice, either. I knew he'd figure it out."

His failure to kill Noah outright showed some remorse. I could capitalize on that. "Noah only wanted what was best for you. He knew that if he helped you, you'd both eventually be caught." That wasn't going to be enough to convince him to let me go. Maybe if I showed him that I'd help him and make up for what he thought I'd taken from him. "If you stop now, I'll testify at your trial and ask for leniency. And the job at Sugarwood will still be yours when you get out."

Oliver laughed—actually laughed—but it sounded more like dry bones rattling together than it did like joy.

There was no way this was going to end well unless I found a way out of this truck.

If I could find something to smash the back windshield... I glanced at it again.

The aqua car was still behind us. It was farther back and small now, but it was definitely still there. Like it was following us the same way Elise had been following me before when she thought I'd had something to do with the attack on Noah. The odds that it was Elise, though, were slim. She had no reason to be spying on me now.

Even if it wasn't Elise, even if it wasn't actually following us, it was a witness, and a witness meant a way out, but I'd have to act before we came to another intersection where that car could turn off.

If I'd shown any skill at all since coming to Fair Haven, it was that I knew how to run a car off the road.

I grabbed the steering wheel and yanked. The truck swerved to the right, and Oliver swore, calling me names that would have made my ever-proper mother punch him in the nose.

The wheels hit the shoulder, and the momentum tugged the car closer to the ditch. I pulled at the wheel again, but Oliver was ready for me this time. He held tight and smashed his fist into the crook of my elbow.

My arm went numb down into my fingers. I lost my grip with that hand.

I wouldn't win against him in a battle of strength.

I let go of the wheel and clawed at his face. The truck jerked left, and then started spinning.

The scream ringing in my ears must have been mine. I doubted Oliver would sound that much like a girl.

The back of the truck smashed into something and flung me sideways as far as the seatbelt would allow. The airbags deployed.

The next thing I knew, the truck had stopped, and I felt dizzy and queasy and like someone had punched me in the face.

*You have to get out of the car*, the voice of reason yelled in my head. *Get out or he'll kill you.*

I released my seatbelt, but all my movements felt too slow and clumsy. Maybe it wouldn't matter. Maybe Oliver had been knocked unconscious.

A hand twisted me around by the hair and shoved me back against the door. Oliver had released his seatbelt as well. Blood ran from the corner of his lip, and one eye was already beginning to swell.

He pinned me with his body weight before I could kick out at him. His hands closed around my neck.

Where was the other car? No one in Fair Haven would see a crash and drive past, would they?

I tried to scream, but I couldn't get air. His fingers dug in, sending lines of pain down my throat and up my neck and into my face. Black stars flickered in my vision. I shoved against him, but he didn't even budge.

And all I could think was that Mark was going to have to autopsy my body and how that might destroy him, too.

Shouting came from outside. A woman's voice.

A woman wouldn't be able to overpower him. He'd kill her, too, and it would be all my fault, like all of this was my fault.

I scratched at his face again, dragging my nails as deep as I could. Instead of letting go, he spit at me and drove his thumbs deeper into my neck. I squeezed my eyes closed. My lungs burned like I was drowning, and the yelling outside faded farther away.

The glass overhead shattered and shards spattered my face along with something wet and warm. Oliver's hands fell away from my neck, and he slumped on top of me, then slid off toward the floor. I gasped in a huge breath, then another. Even that wasn't enough.

The door behind my back dropped away and hands looped under my arm pits.

"Don't look," Elise's voice said. "I'll help you get out. Don't look."

I could guess what had happened and what she didn't want me to see. It wouldn't be the first body, or even the first head shot, I'd witnessed, but I didn't want to see another if I could help it. I kept my eyes closed and relaxed back into her hold as she dragged me out of the car and into the snow. I wasn't in any shape to argue anyway. My throat felt like I'd eaten sand.

"Can you stand up, or do you want to stay put?" Elise asked. "I radioed for help as soon as I saw the truck swerve. That's when I figured it out."

I opened my eyes. She crouched next to me, in her uniform, and the aqua car sat parked in the middle of the street. Her personal car, based on the *Proud Mom of an Honor Student* sticker on the bumper.

I probably could stand, but I wasn't sure I wanted to try yet. The cold snow actually felt good against my undoubtedly bruised body.

Elise sank down into the snow beside me and rested her head back against the truck's fender. "I ordered him to stop, but he wouldn't. I thought he was going to kill you."

The shell-shocked tone to Elise's voice snapped me out of my own bubble. This was her first investigation. If she'd worked in Fair Haven her whole career, it was likely the first person she'd shot, let alone the first person she'd killed.

"You had to do it. He was going to kill me." I slid an arm around her shoulders and ran a hand over my neck where his fingers had gouged my skin. Even the light touch ached. "He was supposed to be taking me to the hospital. He said Noah died. But then once I was in the car, I figured out that he was the one behind everything."

"That's what the hug was about," Elise said, her voice a mixture of comprehension and exhaustion. "The text to Mark was a set up."

So Elise following us hadn't been a coincidence. She had been spying on me, thinking that text spoke the truth. Her distrust had saved my life, but instead of feeling grateful, I felt very alone.

I lowered my arm and scooted sideways a touch. "I wouldn't cheat on Mark."

The daisy chain of events crashed down on me. Oliver sabotaging our sap lines and reverse osmosis machine, injuring Russ and Nancy. Oliver attacking Noah because he refused to help him and then framing Stacey and Tony. Oliver plotting to destroy my relationship with Mark. All of it on my shoulders, and yet none of it truly my fault.

"I didn't even cost Oliver his job at the station. Erik fired him because he violated protocol."

Elise moved close and put her arm around me this time. She smelled like rosemary shampoo, and in a strange way it reminded me of Ahanti, who always smelled like lavender.

"I shouldn't have believed that text," Elise said. "Mark didn't even want to show it to me, but I was there, on my way to work, when it came in, and I grabbed the phone when I saw the look on his face. I've had trouble with trust ever since my ex left, but that's no excuse. I was wrong."

Sirens blared in the distance. If I kept this up, I'd be on a first name basis with the paramedics as well.

I leaned my head into Elise's. I'd take her apology and keep my friend. At least I didn't have to wait for the paramedics alone.

# Chapter 23

I t turned out that Oliver had been telling the truth about Noah's passing. I'd hoped that he'd made that up as well, even though his original plan had been simply to get pictures while taking me to the hospital to see Noah's body. It'd seemed too cold even for Oliver that he'd exploit his cousin's death that way, but he had. I'd never been hated with that level of intensity before.

With Oliver gone, Russ took over arranging Noah's funeral, and he and I split the cost. Mark had invited me to attend the funeral with him and Elise—Meagan and Grant were working, since Cavanaugh's was the only funeral home in town—but I'd thought I should go with the Sugarwood employees. Many of them had known Noah for years, and it felt like I should show solidarity with the ones who hadn't quit us during the trials Oliver created.

Mark and Elise came and stood with our Sugarwood group at the graveside after the service, and Mark took my hand, a public declaration of our new status. I prayed it wouldn't be the last.

With all that'd happened in the past couple of days, I hadn't had a chance to talk to Mark alone about the text Oliver sent, the one that told him I was cheating on him.

The way he stayed by my side suggested he hadn't believed it, but that might simply be because Elise had told him it was a lie rather than because he'd never believed it. I'd experienced more than once that one of Mark's flaws was jealousy, and there was a difference between *I never believed it* and *I believed it until someone told me I shouldn't.* To me, that was an essential distinction.

As everyone left the graveside and headed for their cars, I held Mark back. "We need to talk."

Mark's hold on my hand loosened almost imperceptibly, but I felt it all the way down to my core. "I don't like the sound of that. Do I need to be worried?"

I didn't know how to answer.

I'd had too many people in my life that I couldn't trust, starting with my dad. I knew I could trust Mark—he'd earned it multiple times over—but I also needed him to trust me. Because if he didn't, it said something about the type of person he thought I was. I didn't want him looking at me the way I now looked at my dad.

If he did, it doomed us. If this relationship was going anywhere, he had to be the person in my life who believed the best of me rather than the worst.

Mark dropped my hand completely. "Maybe we should go somewhere else for this conversation."

He mimed to Elise that he was riding with me. We rode in silence, and as we passed through the center of town, I considered driving in circles and apologizing to him and pretending like it didn't matter. I hadn't thought to ask him where we should take the conversation, so I drove us to my house. If this went badly, at least I wouldn't have to drive myself home while crying.

The dogs mobbed us as soon as I let them out of their crates, but they quickly settled in on their doggie beds with their toys.

I motioned Mark to the couch and kept enough distance between us that our legs didn't touch. Past experience had taught me that I didn't think clearly when Mark touched me. I wanted a clear head.

My throat refused to swallow. It felt like I'd tried to eat a pillow whole. "Did you..." My voice hadn't shaken this hard since the last time I tried to speak in front of a jury. "Did you believe the text message that said I was cheating on you?"

The statue-like rigidity in Mark's body relaxed, and he brushed the hair back from my face with the fingers half hidden in the splint for his broken wrist. "That's what you wanted to talk about? I thought you were going to break up with me."

For a second, I forgot what I'd been saying. I'd been in a place before, with Peter, where I let my physical reactions overwhelm my common sense and instincts. I couldn't start another relationship that way. I turned my face away from his touch. "This matters. Elise believed it."

She'd apologized again when we were at the hospital, but it'd still left a sting in my soul. And left me wondering what would have happened to me if she'd written me off and had gone back to tell Mark what she'd seen rather than tagging along to try to get photographic evidence.

"Nikki," Mark's voice was soft, "I know you better than that now. The only reason I believed the rumors about you and Erik was because some of the situations we were in made it seem like you were with him. I never once thought you were involved with Noah or Dave or anyone else." He turned my face back toward him. "I know you better than that."

He gave me that dimpled smile that turned my brain to mush. His gaze dropped to my lips. "But there's still a lot more I'd like to know."

The doorbell rang, and we both jumped.

Mark slumped back against the couch cushions. "It's like we're in a sitcom or something."

The bell rang again, and I hopped up. The jitters running through my body now had nothing to do with fear. The quicker I could deal with whoever was at the door, the better.

I peeked through the peephole. Stacey Rathmell stood on my front steps, one hand twisted in the other.

Part of me wanted to leave her on my steps and go back to the safety of Mark's arms. I was tired of people attacking me, verbally or otherwise.

But that would be the coward's way out.

I opened the door, and Stacey dropped her hands to her sides, stiff like maple trunks.

"I owe you an apology," she said before I could even ask what she was doing here. "I was upset over Noah and my dad, and you didn't deserve it."

One of the things I'd read in Uncle Stan's Bible was that I should forgive people because I'd been forgiven. I didn't want to. When the house was quiet and I was alone, I could still hear her words in my ears, and I had a hard enough time liking myself without anyone else laying indictments at my feet.

I sucked in a deep breath and glanced back over my shoulder at Mark on the couch. He'd turned in the direction of the door, there if I needed him, and the expression on his face was one that said he believed I'd forgive her. It spoke volumes about the kind of person he thought I was. It almost seemed silly that I'd questioned it.

If I didn't forgive her, I'd be one step closer to becoming the person she'd accused me of being and one step farther away from the person Mark saw when he looked at me.

"I forgive you." Somehow saying the words made me feel them a little more. "You were in one of the worst possible positions I could imagine."

She nodded once, sharply. "Thanks."

She walked down the steps. I had the door half closed when she turned around and came back.

The end of her ponytail lay over her shoulder, and she fiddled with the tips of her hair, making her look a lot younger than eighteen.

"I'm pregnant," she blurted. "It's Noah's and I want to keep it. My parents want me to give the baby up for adoption, but I want it. I can handle this."

I held on tight to the doorknob and ordered my mouth not to droop open. I didn't know whether to congratulate her on the new life or console her for how she was going to have to bring it into the world. And a little voice in the back of my head whispered that there was an ask coming.

Stacey huffed in air like she'd forgotten to breathe. "Noah's house is empty now, and you'll want a new mechanic-handyman. I don't know a lot about the stuff you need fixed around here, but I know a lot about cars and I'm a quick learner. I could learn to work the store or the pancake house, too, if you wanted. I'd earn my spot."

I held up my hand to try to slow down the tide of words, but she didn't seem to even see it.

"I don't want to work around the fumes in my dad's shop while I'm pregnant, but I'm going to need a job if I want to keep my baby."

The flow of words stopped abruptly, and she stood there looking much too young to be a soon-to-be single mom on her own. To her credit, she didn't try to guilt me into giving her the job by reminding me that Noah had died protecting me. That show of grace and maturity convinced me that taking her on was the right decision.

Russ was probably going to be cheesed that I'd hired a replacement for Noah without consulting him, but he'd have done the same thing if Stacey asked him. "Will you need help moving your stuff in?"

The way her face lit up burned away any lingering anger or unforgiveness I had toward her. It must have taken a lot for her to humble herself by asking for help from me, who she'd verbally lambasted less than a week ago.

She shook her head, sending her long ponytail swishing. "My dad agreed to help me move, even though this isn't the choice he would have made. My parents love me, and I know they'll love my baby once it's here."

I'd no doubt she was right. Now that I knew she was pregnant, Tony's desire to "make peace" with Noah made more sense. A baby changed everything.

I told Stacey to wait a minute, and I went around behind the door to where Noah's set of keys hung on my key rack. I brought them back and handed them to her. "You can move in as soon as you're ready, and you can start tomorrow if you want."

She dipped her head. "I really appreciate it."

When I closed the door and turned around, Mark stood at the kitchen counter with a plastic container in his hand. He plopped both of our cell phones into it and stuffed it in the fridge.

I stopped on the far side of the kitchen island. "What are you doing?"

Instead of answering, he came around the island, wrapped his uninjured arm around my waist, and kissed me—slow and warm, and better than any of my daydreams.

He finally let me go and grinned down at me. "The phones might have rung. I wasn't taking any more chances."

# Nancy's Make-at-Home Maple Butter

Because of how essential the right temperature is to this recipe, it's a good idea to calibrate your candy thermometer before you start and adjust the temperature in the recipe accordingly.

INGREDIENTS:

1 1/2 cups pure maple syrup

2 tablespoons corn syrup

INSTRUCTIONS:

1. Fill your sink with enough cold water that it will come 1/3 of the way up your pot when you lower the pot into the sink later in the recipe. You don't want your pot to float or water to overflow into your mixture.

2. In a large pot, bring the maple syrup and corn syrup to a boil over medium heat. Stir occasionally. Be careful not to let it burn!

3. Cook the syrup mixture until a candy thermometer reads exactly 232 F (112 C).

4. Remove the pot from the heat, and lower it into the cold water in your sink.

5. Allow the mixture to cool until it reaches 70 F (20 C). This takes about 30 minutes.

6. Remove the pot from the water bath.

7. Using an electric mixer, beat the syrup mixture on high speed until it turns creamy and thick. This takes about 3 minutes. (You'll also want a strong mixer for this step.)

8. Scoop the mixture into a container, cover, and refrigerate for at least two hours before serving.

**Extra Tip:** If the maple butter is too firm to spread straight from the fridge, allow it to come to room temperature before serving.

## LETTER FROM THE AUTHOR

I hope you enjoyed seeing how Nicole solved this mystery (and found out about Mark's wife) as much as I enjoyed writing it. And if you were wishing Nicole's dogs had been around more, they'll be back with a bigger role in *Murder on Tap* (Maple Syrup Mysteries Book 4).

To find out as soon as each new book in the series releases, please sign up for my newsletter at www.smarturl.it/emilyjames.

If you enjoyed *Almost Sleighed*, I'd really appreciate it if you also took a minute to write a quick review wherever you bought the book. Reviews help me sell more books (which allows me to keep writing them), and they also help fellow readers know if this is a book they might enjoy.

Love,
*Emily*

# ABOUT THE AUTHOR

Emily James grew up watching TV shows like *Matlock, Monk,* and *Murder She Wrote.* (It's pure coincidence that they all begin with an **M**.) It was no surprise to anyone when she turned into a mystery writer.

She loves cats, dogs, and coffee. Lots and lots of coffee...lots and lots of cats, too. Seriously, there's hardly room in the bed for her husband. While they only have one dog, she's a Great Dane, so she should count as at least two.

If you'd like to know as soon as Emily's next mystery releases, please join her newsletter list at www.smarturl.it/emilyjames.

She also loves hearing from readers. You can email her through her website (www.authoremilyjames.com) or find her on Facebook (www.facebook.com/authoremilyjames/).

Made in the USA
Coppell, TX
01 December 2020

42608501R00155